P9-DUU-601

THE PIRATE LORD'S WIFE

ANNE R BAILEY

Inkblot Press

Copyright © 2022 by Inkblot Press

All rights reserved.

No part of this book may be reproduced in any form or by any electronic
or mechanical means, including information storage and retrieval
systems, without written permission from the author, except for the use
of brief quotations in a book review.

ALSO BY ANNE R BAILEY

Forgotten Women of History

Joan

Fortuna's Queen

Thyra

Ladies of the Golden Age

Countess of Intrigue

The Pirate Lord's Wife

Royal Court Series

The Lady Carey

The Lady's Crown

The Lady's Ambition

The Lady's Gamble

The Lady's Defiance

Bluehaven Series

The Widowed Bride

Choosing Him

Other

The Stars Above

You can also follow the author at: www.inkblotpressco.ca

CHAPTER 1

1578-1584

Like a thread in a tapestry, my body is wound tight. One wrong movement and I will unravel into a heap of silk, linen, and powder. I glance around the dimly lit gallery. In a few moments the usher will announce me and I will be officially introduced to the queen. Assuming she finds me acceptable, I will become part of her close-knit retinue of ladies with access to her day and night. It's a coveted position that many in the kingdom would kill for.

My whole life I've been preparing for this chance to leap onto centre stage. I cannot falter. My noble ancestors would roll in their graves out of shame if I did. I cannot fail. My beloved brother has sacrificed so much for me to have this chance. I cannot fear. My mother has faced far worse dangers without batting an eye.

The large oak door is cracked open and the usher leans in to listen to the whispered instructions.

This is it. My moment has come.

But my traitorous mind turns away from the future and focuses on the past. All the little events, some contrived, others bartered for, and others mere happenstance that brought me here.

When I was five my father brought me back a fine porcelain doll from France. His mission had been a success and he was full of energy and enthusiasm. At the time, our family had ballooned to a large family of twelve. As the fourth child, I was often overlooked, so when I received such a special gift I treasured it above all my other possessions.

As it happened, I dropped the delicate thing not long after and hid in the garden crying over its broken face and hands. My father discovered me. I like to imagine he had sought me out, but it was far more likely that he simply stumbled across me.

"What sort of creature is filling the evening with such a pitiful sound?"

I looked up to find him crouched down to peer at me underneath the stone bench.

"It's me." I wiped the tears from my eyes.

He looked confused. "I beg your pardon, but I don't know who you are."

"I'm Bess!" My voice began to lose some of its whine. "Your daughter."

Still he did not lose his look of confusion. He shook his head. "Bess? She isn't the sort to be out in the garden at this time of day, and she certainly wouldn't be crying. She's as brave as a lion. If you were Bess you'd know that."

I remember being stunned by his words. With all the stubborn pride of a five-year-old I blurted out, "Yes, I do know. I am Bess and I am brave."

"Then come out from under there. If you want me to believe you, I shall have no more tears out of you."

I pouted but did as he bid. Now frustration and anger had quickly overcome my sadness. By the time I dusted myself off and arranged my clothes, he was looking down at me with a sad sort of smile.

"So what is the matter, little lion? Why have you hidden yourself in the garden?"

I held out my broken doll to him. "It was an accident. I want nothing more than to have this doll back like new again."

He nodded. "May I see?" He peered closer at the doll with the eyes of a trained physician. "Now, little lion cub. All is not lost. The doll may be repaired. It might never be the same doll you once had, but you must learn to love it, cracks and all."

"Truly?"

He laid his hand on my capped head. I remember how it encompassed my whole head, but I wasn't afraid. Then this larger-than-life figure picked me up in one swift movement. "Come along, little lion, back to your den. Your governess has been growing worried."

With my face pressed into the embroidery of his jacket, my mind churned over the realisation that I could be brave. Rewards awaited if I strived to emulate the lion rather than the timid mouse.

The doll was repaired and loved even more.

A year later my father was buried with all solemnity in the family crypt. We, his surviving family, were in shambles. I learned that there would be no money for tutors or pretty dresses. Several of his beautiful estates would have to be sold off as we waited for my brother Arthur to reach his majority.

In a way it was a blessing we didn't have much to our name—not even debts. So we fell prey to neither fortune hunters nor creditors. We were thrilled when my mother was awarded wardship over my brother's lands and knew we could all live together as we had always done. Little did we know my mother's lack of sense when it came to money would bring us to the very edge of ruin.

But in those dark days, we held on to this spark of good news and grew hopeful as we retreated to our last great house: Coughton Court.

No expense was spared on the heir.

Arthur was to have everything and more. He was dressed as well as a duke's son while the rest of us made do with whatever was on hand.

To his credit, it never went to his head. Far from it.

He was ashamed by the favour shown to him by our mother. Since there was no gainsaying her over how she spent the family money, he tried to compensate for her neglect whenever he could.

He took us out to pick walnuts, taught Edward how to ride, helped me puzzle out my letters, and brought treats back for the youngest.

He was an exemplary young man, but to me he was merely a wonderful brother. After a while, I grew to worship him, and I fear I dogged his steps. He was too polite to ever say I annoyed him or that I hindered him far more often than I assisted him.

Compared to other girls, my formal education was scant, so it is Arthur I credit with my education. Having been such an eager pupil meant that in time I was able to repay him for his kindness. I learned far too early to fret over the cost of wheat and read account books. Eventually, I became my brother's eyes and ears whenever he was away from Coughton.

The two of us lived on a prayer and would until he turned twenty-one.

My mother always took his absence as permission for her to run wild with one of her terrible ideas. Only she knew where her machinations were leading, but they never seemed to produce the expected results.

Money was lent freely, but the full sum was never recovered. It's true her money lending could be strategically done. Arthur was able to attend university because of it. But far more often our treasure room and food larders were filled with nothing more than promises of repayment at a later date. When I feared she was getting out of hand, I would send him a missive. He would appear and put a stop to whatever she had planned. Arthur was the only one she would listen to. It was a shame he had to be in London to try to make his way in the world as our father once had.

If my mother suspected I was reporting on her, she never accused me. As her oldest daughter, she had begun to rely on me too. Responsibility after responsibility was hoisted on me, but I took everything in stride.

I wanted to see how far I could go.

Our family home lay nestled in the heart of England, famous for our rose gardens and sprawling parkland. The older I got, the more I grew to appreciate it. Coughton Court was built by my ancestors and looked after with each generation adding more and more to the building. We Throckmortons are an old noble family, though our lineage is not nearly as impressive as others. On that particular day I reminded myself that most of the noble families of England were entwined vines crossing over into each other's plots.

I stood with my pruning shears in hand, examining the rose bush, when from the corner of my eye I caught a glimpse of my mother approaching. She was wearing her black surcoat with an equally dark blouse beneath. It was the height of summer; she must have been sweltering underneath all that black damask. At the time, she was still playing the part of the grieving widow. My father, God rest his soul, had died seven years ago, and even though she was still young she had no plans to marry yet. Maybe no one wanted the responsibility that came with her.

"Bess, what are you doing out here in the middle of the day?"

"I hadn't realised so much time had passed." A wide-brim hat covered my face and the long sleeves of my blouse protected my arms. I had not felt the heat of the sun.

Behind me a line of rose bushes, a new variety we had been breeding, were all neatly trimmed. Only one on the edge of the row needed my attention.

My mother examined my handiwork and nodded approvingly.

"I didn't want them to grow too wild."

"I can see that." Then she sighed. "But really, Bess, I shouldn't be allowing you out here. What gentlewoman's daughter spends her time outdoors digging in the dirt? You should be inside working on your accomplishments."

I bit back a laugh. "There's plenty of time for that in the winter. The gardeners have their work cut out for them already. This new variety deserves my special attention."

I removed my thick leather glove to stroke the petals of the flower. They were a brilliant white with a streak of red in the middle.

"Do you think they will please the queen?"

"Certainly," my mother said with a sniff. "She likes

everything new and fine. Once enough have bloomed, we shall send her bouquets and perhaps she will think kindly of us."

I could feel one of her fits of despair coming, so I changed the topic. "Is it true that Arthur will be joining us?"

"Yes, your brother has remembered that we exist."

"Oh, Mother. He loves us very much. You know he's just called away by circumstance."

My mother shook her head ruefully. "He is avoiding me."

I began to lead her back inside. Internally, I knew she was not wrong, but I didn't want to confirm her fears.

"He knows I want to see him married and settled down here at Coughton. Yet he insists on ignoring my advice."

"Serving the queen is how he will make his fortune."

"Is it now? He's nearly twenty-five! Your father and I had been well settled in our married life and had plenty of children to fill the nursery by that age. I fear everything will be lost if your brother doesn't do his duty."

My mother's main goal in life was to see us all married. I was only grateful that my own betrothal to a local gentleman never went through. My father had been set on making the alliance with his dear old friend. But Henry Tadius was a pudgy youth, with small beady eyes and a terrible temper. My mother intervened, and with her assistance and my terribly low dowry, that marriage prospect was put off. By all standards I was still young, so I didn't want to be swallowed up by the dull life in the country. I loved my home and my family for all their faults, but when I closed my eyes I dreamed of the glittering court and London. I drooled at the thought of all the pretty clothes, the dances and music. Surely, fate would take me on a grand adventure. But even my very meagre reading told me that fate was a cruel mistress. Nothing stopped me from dreaming. Or being jealous of my favourite sibling. "I think he likes his life at court. He sits in parliament and he's well respected by Cecil. Perhaps..."

My mother let out the most dramatic sigh. "You two were always thick as thieves. I should not expect to hear a sympathetic word from your quarter."

My back stiffened. She was wrong. It wasn't always just Arthur and me. We had Edward and Margaret to plot alongside us. The four of us got into all sorts of mischief, but when the smallpox swept through the village and the whole household seemed afflicted, they succumbed to the fever. As Arthur was often away from home, I was the oldest and took up the mantle of acting as my mother's second-in-command.

"Now, Mother. Really. Come, let's go inside and you can tell me all about the grand marriage prospects you found for Arthur."

We made it to the great hall, where most of the household was assembled. A quick scan of the room told me that my younger siblings had been tucked away in the schoolroom with their tutor. My next two youngest sisters were working on painting a screen together, and they seemed to be arguing over the composition of the piece.

They looked up when we came in and rearranged their expressions into ones of contentment. This might have fooled my mother, but I raised an eyebrow at them.

The steward was with our chamberlain looking over our accounts and calculating what would be needed to repair the roof before winter.

Coughton Court had lacked the funds to keep up with maintenance over the last few years. Both the steward and chamberlain resented my mother, who enjoyed spending money lavishly. She threw it around as if it were easy to come by. I knew that they too dreamed of Arthur settling down and taking over the running of the household from my mother. They saw him as a prudent young man who would save the house from the financial woes my mother was keen on putting us in.

I could not help but frown at the disloyalty.

She was entitled to live a comfortable life. What would people say if we didn't have the very best? Why would our tenants respect us if they were dressed in finer clothes than us?

"There is a matter I wish to speak to you about, Bess," my mother said, leading me to the oriel window. Her hand on my arm was tense and I felt the same rigidity spread throughout my own body as well.

Had my fears come true? Had someone asked for my hand in marriage?

"Remember when the Earl of Huntingdon stopped here for a short sojourn?"

"I do." I nodded.

"Well, he wrote to me not long after. He loved our

little home. I didn't think to correct him by telling him that Coughton has a larger park than the queen's own Hatfield House. Besides, I can imagine that his own is indeed much finer." She caught my look of irritation.

"Don't worry, dearest. I'm getting to the point." She laughed. "I forget how impatient the young are these days. How is anything going to get done in the kingdom? I cannot imagine. Well, he offered me the chance to participate in an interesting proposition. A business venture."

Even as young as I was I knew what this meant. "He asked you for a loan?"

"He promises to pay me back as soon as the ship returns from the New World."

"Oh, Mother. How much?"

She waved her hands. "It was nothing. Just five hundred pounds."

I gape. "Where did such a sum come from?"

"Well, it was to be your inheritance from your father."

It took a great effort to ignore the pinprick sensation of anger travelling up my arm. "But..."

"He will repay us, and he has promised that he will return the favour and even allow us to participate in his next venture."

"How generous." There was a bite to my words that she noticed.

"You will see. Mark my words, Bess, this is for the best. Besides, we are growing a list of allies and connections. Who knows, maybe the earl will single you out as a prospective for one of his sons." She examined me with those piercing blue eyes I wished I had inherited. In her day, she had been a great beauty. "You are certainly comely enough."

"Thank you." I had no pretensions or designs on my looks. They served a purpose, but I had enough brains to realise that they faded with time.

"Now your sister Beatrice. She will make a great match with that golden hair and my blue eyes..." Mother stopped to examine her favourite daughter—the one who resembled her the most. "We really must do something for her."

I offer, if only to get the topic away from myself: "I'm sure the house will be crawling with suitors when she is of age."

"Hmm. You are right. I never have to fear for her future." The wistful sound in my mother's voice ended when she clicked her tongue on the roof of her mouth. "I better go stop the two of them. They look ready to fight. Beatrice and Mary are inseparable but go from one extreme to another in a moment."

I caught the younger of the two pinching the other. "Mary certainly knows how to irritate Beatrice."

I was left at the window to gaze out to the gravelled courtyard. Any anger and resentment toward my mother had already left me. By now I had learned to be resigned in order to save my sanity. I knew this was wrong but... what more could a girl like me ask for?

When I was a child, I was required to write out the mottos of all the kings and queens that came before. It made me think about what my own motto would be. I had settled upon: *The gentler course.* It suited me. Thus far, it had served me well and dulled the sting of disappointment. The way I saw it, I was powerless no matter what, so the less I fought, the greater the chance I would have to be content and untroubled. Being amenable was my dominant trait, far more than my wit, loyalty, or even appearance. I always went where life would take me, refusing to fight the current. What could I do to stop it anyway?

I heard the raised voice of the steward on the other side of the room. He meant for Mother to hear him complaining, but I knew she would ignore him and press on with her plans.

Arthur arrived like a tempest wind on the sea threatening to capsize our ship. He embraced me warmly, but to our mother he reserved only cold respect.

"My son." Her eyes narrowed into the slits of an angry barn cat. "Are you not well?"

He handed off his cloak to a waiting servant. Arthur had picked up new habits, and the way he took off his cloak and pulled off his riding gloves was done with thought and grace. He'd spent his time in London learning the fashionable customs and behaviours that were totally alien to me to gain favour with the queen.

"We shall speak in private," he said to her.

"As you wish," she sniffed.

He looked at me and tried to find a smile. "I have brought you and all our sisters some presents from London."

I returned the gesture with a small curtsy. I tried to let him know that I'd much rather attend his little meeting with Mother. His head gave the smallest of shakes. No. I accepted this in good measure. If he were inclined to, he would let me know what happened in time. And if not, then I would barter for the knowledge. I might have accepted what life threw my way, but that didn't mean I wasn't wily enough to get what I wanted.

The presents from London were starched ruffs for us three older sisters to wear. They were done up in the latest fashion and the lace was so fine it was almost transparent.

I oohed and aahed over this extravagant gift along with my other sisters, while at the same time watching them to make sure they didn't accidentally ruin them.

"I shall have these tucked away for special occasions."

"But..." Beatrice pouted. "I'd like to wear mine now."

"And if it gets ruined? You shall not have another."

"Arthur will get me more." Beatrice moved on to frowning. Her lower lip quivered. I could see that she was about to cry. That might have been enough to convince Mother, but she would find me far more indifferent.

"He will not. There is no money. So cheer up. Why don't you take Mary and go for a walk in the garden? The two of you are cooped up indoors too often."

"We are careful with our complexions," Beatrice said with an impetuous toss of her head.

I merely shrugged as I set about placing the ruffs back into their protective coverings and instructed the maid to tuck away the boxes far out of the reach of my sisters.

It was after supper and the family had retreated to the privacy of my father's old study hall. Couches, divans, and padded chairs littered the room with toys and books scattered about.

This room was never shown to those outside the family. It was somewhere we could go to retreat and enjoy the pleasure of each other's company. Today it felt quite different. There was a tension in the air that made even the youngest of us silent.

My mother was busy reading from a book of psalms while Arthur was tapping his foot and staring at the flames in the grate as if he was wishing himself anywhere but here.

"Shall I play the lute for us?"

The pair of them nearly jumped in their seats.

"What an excellent idea," my mother said.

Arthur nodded. "If it would please you."

The governess handed me the lute and I struck a chord, testing the instrument. Happy to see it was still in tune, I began a song. The last time I had seen my brother he had brought music sheets from London, and by now I had learned them by heart. I hoped it pleased him. He was certainly regarding me with a studious eye.

When he caught me watching him, he smiled and gave me an approving nod.

Once I was done I offered the lute to Mary, who was fond of the instrument, and let her have her turn.

"You've improved a lot," Arthur said, inviting me to sit between him and our mother.

"I do occasionally try to excel at something."

He laughed and I grinned in turn, but my attention was fixed on Mother on my left. She'd turned herself away from the two of us but occasionally cast a dark glance toward my brother.

I met Arthur's gaze, arching my eyebrow.

A mixture of emotions crossed his face until he seemed to settle on one in particular. Resignment.

He cleared his throat. "I have news for you."

Had he and Mother quarrelled over me? Was that what was going on? My heart began to hammer in my chest as I waited for my brother to find the courage to defy our indomitable mother.

"After the new year I shall come to bring you to court. You have been offered a position in her majesty's court."

My mouth fell open at the impossibility of all my wildest dreams coming true.

"Would you accept?"

"Of course she will." My mother interrupted before I had time to answer. "She'd be a fool not to. Besides, she's been dreaming of this moment for years." She shook her head as if the idea was displeasing to her.

My brother and I shared a look.

Our family history was steeped in intrigue and death. I grew up learning to be ashamed of my maternal grand-father. He had been executed as a traitor alongside four other men accused of being Anne Boleyn's lovers. Of course, this was nothing but false rumours. However, no one can ever be sure, and this stain on our reputation will follow us forever.

It was not enough, however, to keep my own mother from being invited to come to court.

I glanced back to the left, studying my mother's profile. Even at her advanced age I could see how her equal features and soft rounded eyes would have been pleasing. She had a tendency to brag about how her dazzling prettiness drew everyone's attention, including the king's. Some say the king did more than just admire her. Not that my mother has ever confirmed anything. To be fair, this would hardly have been a suitable subject to discuss with your own children.

Despite this, I knew that there were more than a few jewels in my mother's possession that could only have come from one man.

"I would like to come serve the queen more than anything in the world," I said, turning to Arthur. "How is it possible that this has come about?"

"I'm happy to hear that. Serving the queen is an enormous responsibility, but I think it is one you will learn to appreciate. It's not all needlework and playing."

I nodded my head, mimicking his serious expression.

"There are also many who would be more than happy to replace you."

"I know. Everyone wants to be around the queen..."

"It's more than that. You must see this, Bess." He

leaned forward, speaking low. "You will be privy to information. Valuable information."

My mind, so focused on my own happiness, took a moment to let his words sink in. Being a maid of honour to the queen would mean I would finally have something to barter. Money would be pressed into my hands. Assuming, of course, I could play my cards right.

"So how come I have been singled out?"

"I have called in a favour with the Earl of Huntingdon," Arthur said, not bothering to hide his discontentment from our mother. "He will ensure you have a place at court since he has taken away your chance at a respectable marriage."

My mother looked ready to reprimand him, but she held back.

After the new year, Arthur escorted me to London, but our plans did not go off as smoothly as we had imagined.

There was no official opening for me anymore. The cloud of suspicion had fallen on our family, as my aunt had been caught writing letters to the disgraced Scottish Queen Mary. Suddenly the Throckmortons had a new stain on their name. My aunt was executed for her plotting, but neither my brother nor I shed a tear.

Our own personal views were held locked away in a secret compartment of our hearts. We were raised in a Catholic household, during King Edward's day when it was forbidden to hear the Mass. We hid away priests in our store cupboards and passed along messages to our Catholic allies overseas.

Regardless of how we might feel now, it would never be forgotten who we supported and what we had done. Certainly not by this queen and not by her councillors. It was said that Cecil carried a journal on his person where he wrote down the names of all suspected Catholics and sympathisers alike. The English people were waging a silent war among themselves. Factions popped up as frequently as they disappeared.

At the moment it was the Protestants and the queen in the ascendency.

Perhaps my brother and I were turncoats, disloyal to our family and upbringing. But we were survivors first and foremost, so I didn't question him when he took me to hear the English liturgy.

A year passed but my time in London was not wasted. Arthur had not taken me under his wing to be reliant on him forever. As once I followed my brother around, I now dogged the steps of the noble ladies of the court. I was always there as a helpful shadow, undaunted by the tasks they might demand of me. I didn't have the pride of the other noble ladies to find serving them beneath me.

In time they came to appreciate me. I learned to make myself indispensable while at the same time I collected any information that came my way. This was how I learned courtly manners, how to write in code and decode a letter. I learned my way around the bustling palaces.

It was not always an easy apprenticeship. The queen preferred to be the primary woman at court. The gentlemen of her realm left their wives and daughters at home in the country. So often there was little for me to do since I had not been admitted to the queen's rooms personally.

I had seen her from afar many times. Once I had sat in a box at the theatre within sight of her and yet she never acknowledged me, though I was sure after so many years at court she must have known of me.

My brother promised that soon things would be different.

But I could see something preoccupied him. The way he got distracted every time Lady Ann Lucas entered the room made me wonder how soon it would be before we would have a wedding and a new mistress at Coughton Court.

The tide of fortune began to shift one day when I volunteered to fetch Lady Burghley's prayer book from her rooms. I was halfway back to the gardens when I found myself face-to-face with her husband, the great councilman himself.

I curtsied low and politely to him but waited for him to speak first.

"Good day, Lady Bess. Don't let me keep you from your duties."

I came up from my curtsy and bravely met his gaze. "You could never do so, my lord."

He chuckled and caught a glimpse of what was in my hands. "My lady wife employs enough pages to not have to send you scampering about."

"It brings me joy to be of use." I kept my eyes downcast now.

"I'm sure it does. None of us have failed to notice how you've made yourself a busy bee around court. Don't let me keep you any longer."

I had not known at the time, but Arthur had spoken to Cecil about either finding a match for me or a place at court.

I could not know what Cecil gleaned from this brief interview, but the very next week a marriage proposal was put before me.

"It is a good match," Arthur said. "The best you could hope for under the circumstances."

"I am sure he is a fine gentleman with a good home, but he is not for me." By then I had become determined that nothing would keep me from court. I would become one of the noble ladies that were given the honour of serving the queen.

Arthur frowned and rubbed a hand over his chin. He was growing a beard, but the hair was so fine it looked patchy in places. I suggested he shave it off, but he'd been stubborn. A certain lady my brother fancied had been reported as having said she preferred bearded men. I dropped the subject but couldn't help but laugh at how foolish being in love made him.

Nothing was settled until weeks later when my mother came to my aid. She agreed with me that the match was not good enough for me to give up all chance of joining the queen's service. I might not have had a dowry but I carried an ancient noble lineage in my veins. That was still worth something. I had also learned that those who served the queen had better chances. She often stepped in to provide dowries and arranged fabulous marriages for her ladies.

In the end, we forced my brother to give way. Thoughts of marriage were put aside.

Knowing that Cecil had arranged it all, I hoped he wasn't upset.

I had my answer a few days later. When my brother pulled me aside to inform me that Cecil wished to speak to me about a position in her majesty's household, I wondered if this had been a test all along.

Cecil's office, with its wood panelling and roaring fire, made me feel cocooned in warmth and safety.

He alternated between looking at the ledger and up at me as if judging where I might fit best.

"You are a headstrong young lady. The queen will

appreciate your strength of character. It is not always easy serving her, as I'm sure you've heard."

"I would never expect anything to be easy," I offered, trying to reassure him of my willingness to learn.

He hummed in reply, pushing back the spectacles on his eyes. "Tensions are high at the moment between our Catholic subjects and Protestant. I will be blunt with you. This is the primary reason I have singled you out. We need to show—balance in her majesty's household."

"But I am not..."

He held up a hand. "Regardless of your true feelings on the subject, you are associated with the latter group. Don't fret. I know you have no political leanings nor entertain taking part in any Catholic intrigues. Yet another reason you are suitable for this post."

The blood had drained from my face.

When he looked up, he could clearly see my distress. "I take it you shall not give me any cause for concern. Correct?"

"No, my lord."

"Good."

The rest of the interview was a blur, and now, a week later, I am here waiting for the usher to let me through to the queen's presence chamber beyond.

I straighten up as he looks at me and with a nod motions for me to come.

I glide forward toward my future.

L ady Hastings drapes a beige cloth over my shoulder before stepping back to consider me.

"Far too drab."

I finger the delicate fabric. It's soft and catches the light, but I can foresee that in the evening it will become plain.

"Perhaps if this was a daytime performance, then it would be suitable," I say, glancing around the room. We are in one of the queen's many galleries, filled with varying degrees of fabrics and dresses. An emerald green catches my eye. "What about that one?"

Lady Hastings follows my gaze. "That one? You are to be a sea nymph, not a forest dryad."

"Throw some blue gauze on top. The sea is not all one colour."

She arches her eyebrow, but there is a reason the queen has instructed me to assist with this task. I have an eye for these sorts of things.

Ever since I came into her service I have tried to make myself useful to her. Unfortunately, I am not a great wit or musician, nor do I know any foreign language beyond some rudimentary French. However lacking my education has been, I have not let this stop me.

We sort out the rest of the costumes for the other four ladies and try to figure out which colours would be complementary to our male counterparts.

Lady Hastings is digging through some trimming when I catch a glimpse of a bolt of black cloth.

It's a heavy velvet with a deep, even colour. However, as I test the fabric my light touch makes the fabric shed. The quality is clearly lacking, but for our purposes it might suit.

"I think capes for the men made out of this would be our best option." I pull on the bolt with a sharp tug.

"Black?"

"Yes," I say with a mischievous smile. "The ladies should be the focal point of the play anyway. We could line the interior of the capes with shining silver if you think that it would be too plain otherwise."

Lady Hastings contemplates what I've said and then at last nods. "Brilliant. Far too often the men go around strutting around like peacocks, stealing all the attention from us."

"It doesn't help that we are outnumbered," I say. Despite having a queen on the throne of England, men far outnumber the women at her court. Considering how much she enjoys the spotlight, this is understandable. Though she enjoys surrounding herself with beauty and perfection, the queen prefers that her ladies fade into the background.

The news from abroad has been bad and the queen's mood equally foul. In an effort to cheer her, we are putting on a play at the behest of one of her favourites, Charles Blount. It is amusing to watch the men fight over her favour. Usually it would be Leicester ordering such fetes, but alas for the queen, he is abroad leading the English army in the Netherlands.

Despite our united efforts, the Spanish are better equipped and led. They aren't limited by costs or men they have available. It feels like we are losing a battle we never could've won. But we try to keep our spirits up and pretend like nothing is wrong.

We return to the maids' chamber with our findings. Our compatriots drift around the room like white clouds.

Lady Hastings is put out.

"What is happening here?" she asks, grabbing Catherine Howard, nee Carey, the queen's cousin and favoured companion as she walks by.

Being a mother of a large brood, she doesn't take kindly to the jolting, questioning way she is interrupted.

"The queen has changed her mind and will dine in public this evening." She pauses to stop another girl passing by to adjust her sleeves before turning back to us with a look of decided annoyance. "With the French ambassador."

She doesn't need to clarify what this means. For official court functions we are all required to dress in the gowns the queen gifted us. All white velvet with gold trimmings. None of us will stand out. Except perhaps Mary Knollys, who happens to be the shortest of us.

Someone else brushes past Catherine and her eyes narrow. She's off muttering about the rudeness of young people.

I watch her move in and out of the crowd, her critical eyes missing nothing. I might envy her confidence and the position of favour she holds in the queen's household if it wasn't for the lonely path she treads. At thirty-eight, she's in an awkward position of having no one her own age for company. The rest of us are either two decades older or younger than her. In lieu of friends, she's taken on the task of overseeing the younger maids and takes her job seriously.

Catherine Carey is one of the few the queen can rely on, and she trusts her to keep us on our best behaviour. The queen wants no whisper of scandal in her court. The whole world knows Queen Elizabeth I is a virgin queen. However, considering her tendency to give visiting dignitaries glimpses of her bare breasts—always accidentally of course—or flirt so brazenly with her favourites, she can't be surprised that we indulge ourselves in unseemly behaviour as well.

Some perhaps too much.

It causes Catherine endless headaches and I suspect her face will be set in a permanent frown forever. I was given the opportunity to serve the queen only because one such lady was banished from court for overstepping the boundary of courtly love. Dorothy, the sister of the Earl of Essex, had been too free with her favours, and the result was a haystack wedding conducted in secret. When the queen discovered this, Dorothy found herself exiled in disgrace.

Unlike some, I cannot bring myself to sneer at her for making a decision without thinking of her family or even her own reputation and future. Instead, I often daydream of being in her position. The idea is both ludicrous and appealing. Allowing myself the freedom to follow my own desires leaves a taste so sweet on my tongue that I find it hard to swallow. In the next breath, I come crashing back down to earth as I remember there is a difference between dreams and reality. Is it possible for me to love someone so much that I could forget myself in such a way?

A serving woman approaches, bowing to the both of us.

"We have your clothes ready for you, my ladies," she says, keeping her eyes downcast.

Lady Hastings and I retreat behind heavy curtains to change. We strip down to our smocks, and the layers differentiating us melt away. Our matching petticoats with bodices, delicate roses embroidered in gold thread, are laced tightly before the skirt is put on over the top. We tie up our stockings with the same white garters before our feet disappear into equally white slippers. The dresses are elegant but not flattering. Across from me, Lady Hastings has become my mirror image. Even the gold chains pinned to our bodices and the ruffs and cuffs added to our sleeves are the same. Then on goes the farthingale and heavy gown on top. Over the years, I have grown used to its hindering weight, but I often dream of the simpler dresses I wore at Coughton.

The maids come forth with girdles, fans, handker-chiefs, gloves, and delicate ropes of pearls.

All these items are on loan from her majesty's coffers.

"I'll trade you for yours," Lady Hastings says, holding out her pearls.

Our eyes meet and we hazard a laugh.

Her fingers graze the pearls, examining them for a fault. There will be none, but she stops at one that is discoloured.

"This shall have to be replaced," she instructs the maid waiting nearby. The queen expects perfection.

We exit the dressing area and join the throng of ladies. The first time I saw the parade of her ladies in these dresses I was both dazzled and blinded by all the white. It felt impossible to pick out a single person in the crowd. Now my eyes have become trained to focus on the minute details that separate each lady. It grows harder as our faces are painted and powdered, further obscuring our features. Our hair is pinned up in exactly the same way. Finally, headdresses covered in seeded pearls complete our elaborate ensembles.

We wear a fortune on our backs to honour our mistress and to flaunt England's wealth. As the outfit is both uncomfortable and makes us resemble ghosts, I am grateful it is rare for us to actually march out in our state clothing.

"You are looking well." Lady Anne Holland has

sidled up next to me. We will be walking according to precedence, and she is always my walking partner.

"As are you." I tilt my head to compliment her. Even with the face powder I can see the flush in her cheeks and her bright eyes that always draw attention. "What were you doing while Lady Hastings and I were digging around the storeroom?"

She gives me a half-smile, and her eyes flash with excitement at the secret she carries close to her chest.

"I was here on my best behaviour."

"Why do I find that hard to believe?"

"I am sure I have no idea what you are trying to imply." She wears an impish smile, as if eager for me to press her for more information. But just like that, the master of ceremony comes in and clears his throat. As one we straighten up, ready to play our parts.

Dinner is course after course of exotic dishes. The rich food tends to turn my stomach, but I am too aware of the eyes watching us all. We sit below the queen at her head table but above the courtiers and lower nobility dining below.

If I crane my head just right, I get a good view of the queen, who is sitting under the canopy of estate. Tonight she is decked in one of the magnificent gowns she saves for court paintings. The thin gauze butterfly wings that frame her face are so large tonight that it looks as if they might swallow her whole.

On her left is the Earl of Leicester, Robert Dudley, recently returned from the Netherlands. On her right the French ambassador, whose soft grey eyes hide a viper. Our queen is eager to make an alliance with the French.

Not long ago she accepted a marriage proposal from one of their own—well, almost. By the next day she had told him she was forced to refuse after all. The Duke of Anjou had died just a year ago, and in remembrance of her frog the queen ordered us into full mourning. I had not met him myself, but plenty at court had. After his death many ladies spoke fondly of him. He had not been handsome in the conventional way, but he had a way with words and was unapologetically brash. He was the only man to have been so close to marrying the queen.

The ambassador leans toward her to whisper something. I watch how he carefully avoids letting his gaze fall lower than her lips to the low decolletage of her gown.

It would give the queen satisfaction if he did look. She adores male attention, which she has always used as a weapon against them. Perhaps he knows and is withholding on purpose. He catches me watching him and there's a spark of amusement in his eye as he inclines his head ever so slightly. A movement anyone else observing could have missed. Like I thought, he's a viper. Certainly, he's not even bothering to pretend to be entranced by the queen as he's supposed to be.

Queen Elizabeth is undaunted. I am certain she is simply recalculating the sum she is going to bribe him with to earn his smile. In the past, all she had to do was hint that she wished to marry—a far cheaper tactic for

England's coffers. But alas for us all, she is no longer of marriageable age.

In contrast, Robert Dudley does not hesitate to play the besotted suitor. Their relationship has gone on longer than I've been alive. By all accounts, it was a long journey for him to get here. There were many times when he too could have married her. They still play their coquettish games, but the passion behind their actions has cooled into friendship. I can see why too. He has grown pudgy, his hairline has receded, and his once handsome face is lined after years of service to the queen. The last few years he has added gout to his list of maladies. The heavy rich food he favours has not helped his worsening health.

Though there is an alternate rumour that hints his bad constitution is his wife's doing. It would not be the first time Lettice Knollys has been accused of poisoning her husband.

Her first, the Earl of Essex, died suddenly one day. The couple had a tumultuous relationship. If her son, Robert Devereux didn't look like the spitting image of her husband, his parentage would be in doubt. The earl was threatening to divorce her and challenged Dudley to a duel before his untimely end. It caused quite a stir. Everyone was certain she had slipped something in his drink but the queen waved it off as rumours. When a few months later a pregnant Lettice married her lover, Dudley, the court was scandalised. Who was the father?

Having lived so often at court, I have learned that one's parentage is hardly a guarantee. Luckily, there is no way to tell unless the couples are caught in the act so more often than not we turn the other cheek. When the Earl of Nottingham arrives at court bearing a strong resemblance to the Count of Ferrier and not his own father, no one says a word.

Is it any surprise that in a world where marriages are purely for the sake of alliances couples seek comfort elsewhere?

Even Robert Dudley, who married Lettice in a moment of passion and necessity no longer tolerates her presence.

Love is fickle. I must remember to steel my heart against it.

I turn my attention back to my plate. The venison dripping in a thick roux and seasoned with saffron and nutmeg does nothing to whet my appetite. I reach instead for a slice of bread and pick at it.

After the dishes are cleared away, tables are cleared out of the way to make room for the entertainment. First there is a short tableau put on by Charles Blount. The imagery is clear, St. George slaying the dragon. Judging by the dragon's red and orange scales, this is a thinly veiled allusion to Spain.

Despite the elaborate dragon costume that breathes fire and draws gasps from those around me, it is St. George who captures my attention—and holds it. I recognise him at once as Sir Walter Raleigh, a man with a dark reputation for debauchery. He stands ready with a blue shield shamelessly painted with a fleur-de-lis on it. Once all eyes are on him, he salutes the queen and gives the French ambassador a mischievous grin. The music is timed perfectly with his movements. The decorative sword polished within an inch of its life catches the candlelight as he swishes it in mock battle with the dragon. Just as the music crescendos, he manages to pierce its heart. Black ribbons spew from the dragon. We all applaud.

I find myself studying Raleigh as he removes his halo and shakes out his dark hair. His hair, left to grow long, is curled as if he has taken a hot iron to it. He is known for his vanity and flamboyant style, so I wouldn't put it past him. With the dragon vanquished, he performs his bow to the queen with a flourish, and she nods to him and commends his graceful performance.

Graceful isn't the word I would've used. But maybe that's because all I could focus on was the taut shape of his calf as he sprang around and the glint in his green eyes as he thrust toward the dragon—dangerous even in this act of play. I can see why the man has developed a bad reputation. Even the kindest of his friends would say he is a notorious explorer and philanderer. His enemies call him a pirate and a cad.

All this means nothing because the queen favours him and has not sent him away from court. He's useful and good at what he does. But I can see the restlessness in the set of his shoulders as he retreats from the great hall to change.

Next a pair of acrobats hop on to centre stage, making the crowd laugh as one of them trips the other and they tumble to the floor in a sprawling mess.

However, I am watching the door. Perhaps it is foolish, but when Raleigh steps through again, sliding back through the crowd to be at Cecil's side, I cannot help but admire the handsome outfit he has changed into. There's a gorget around his neck etched with silver gilt and a cape of midnight blue. His carefully selected pieces make him all the more handsome, but it's that mischievous glint in his eyes that makes heat pool in the pit of my stomach the longer I watch him.

Enough. I force myself to look away. The last thing I need is for someone to notice my attention on him.

As the night drags on, we ladies dance for the court. I am partnered with Lady Holland, as the two of us are of similar height, and we twirl around the room.

"You are distracted this evening," she comments.

"Nonsense. Just tired."

She doesn't believe me, but she cannot question me further as the dance requires all of our focus.

I have seen this dance performed before. We are meant to look like a cloud of apple blossoms carried by a summer breeze. When we spin in the arms of our partners our dresses are on display for the glorification of our queen and country. We dazzle and enchant.

Then when the song ends we retreat and let others take to the dance floor.

This whole time the queen has been tapping her fingers in time with the music but also speaking to the ambassador in a hushed tone.

Whatever she has been saying seems to have won him over. He is leaning closer to her, his features softened by his smile.

She motions to the server behind them, who comes forward to refill their glasses with expensive Bordeaux wine that the queen knows is his favourite. They make a private toast between the two of them.

She's captured him.

Our queen has rarely failed in this regard. Whether people love or hate her, when they are in her presence they cannot help but hang on her every word. She's an enigma in this world and no one quite knows what to make of her—even her friends.

I study Robert Dudley, who is pretending not to care that his onetime love is flirting with another man. His movements are poised, but I catch the way his eyes dart to the queen when she throws her head back to laugh at something the ambassador says, her hand touching the exposed decolletage and drawing every-one's eyes to the swell of her bosom. Dudley's expres-sion slips and his eyes narrow as he looks past her to the ambassador, who has placed a kiss on her naked palm.

In any other situation it would be considered uncouth for a woman of her advanced years to be acting so shamelessly. But she isn't just any woman. She is a queen. The queen. It helps her illusion of desirability that she has retained her lithe figure, and rigorous exer-cise has ensured she is still spry.

Then she surprises us all by getting to her feet.

We stop to watch with bated breath as her fingers caress Robert's shoulder. He stands, bowing to her and offering her his arm. A maid springs forward and with practiced ease removes the butterfly wings that would have impeded her.

She places her hand in his. We all catch the way his thumb grazes the top of her hand. They don't exchange a single word. They don't need to.

Dudley leads her to the dance floor. The way is cleared and with a nod from her the music begins: a spirited galliard.

As they take their positions the pair is transformed. As they twirl and jump, years melt away and I can imagine them as they must have been when she was twenty-six and newly crowned. His touch lingers, hers is daring. Her eyes are alight with desire as her lips part when he lifts her off the ground.

Her gown is shown to full effect now. The vibrant red silk and diamonds sewn into the fabric send shards of light dancing around the room as she spins.

My eyes travel around the room and settle back on Walter Raleigh. He is speaking to Cecil, but at that very moment he looks up. Our eyes meet. For a moment I think I will look away, but then I cannot bring myself to be so cowardly. I give him a small nod, which he returns, and force myself to move on.

I hope it's enough to show him that I wasn't singling him out. A man with his reputation isn't one I should be drawing the attention of.

The music stops and there is silence before a burst of applause from the courtiers.

We, her ladies, know her well, and though her skin is flushed and she looks ready for another dance, we can tell that she is tired. There is a slight waver in her hand as she straightens up, and she looks like she is forcing herself to keep her breath steady. Perhaps she could push herself through another set, but glancing at Lady Holland on my right, I can see I am not the only one who thinks it would be best if she returns to her seat.

The French ambassador is on his feet, applauding the loudest.

"Magnifique," he calls out in his native French before snapping for his own servant to come forth with a gift.

Robert Dudley leads the queen back up to the dais to accept it.

Being so close, I can see the chain of emeralds as the lid off the chest is opened. They are sitting on a muff of sable fur. It's a generous gift. One that will surely please the queen.

She nods appreciatively over the cut of the emeralds and assures the ambassador that the sable is the softest she has ever felt.

Queen Elizabeth returns to her seat and the ambassador to his. Every word and gesture will be reported throughout Christendom by the other ambassadors and foreigners gracing the court today. This display of friendship between the English and French has been the greatest show of pageantry of all. We can only pray it is enough to scare off the Spanish.

By the time I find my way to my bed I am ready to collapse.

Exhaustion overwhelms me. A chorus of "good nights" begins and, not wishing to be rude, I add my weak voice for good measure. My head sinks into the down-filled pillow, but I don't fall into the sweet embrace of sleep. Rather, my mind lingers on a pair of fine green eyes.

~

With any free time we have, we have been practicing for the masque that will be performed for the queen to kick off the Christmas festivities.

However, this is a strangely tepid day for this late in November. A ride followed by a picnic in the woods is arranged by Raleigh, standing in for the missing Master of Horse. A large party, myself included, is heading toward the established meeting place.

On my head is a new green velvet hat, gifted to me by my generous brother. It's decorated with the white plume of an ostrich feather and a silver buckle, which adds an air of sophistication to it. I suspect that it wasn't my brother who selected this piece as a gift for me but rather his betrothed. It fills me with joy to think that soon he will have his heart's desire. He finally brokered a marriage contract between our two families, and come spring, Lady Ann will wed him.

Long before talks of contracts began, however, they had fallen in love. I always wonder what finally won her over, but there are some topics even I don't dare tread on.

My horse, a borrowed gelding from the royal stables, flounders, and I have to pull back to let others pass. I pat his neck reassuringly and let him follow behind at his own pace.

The queen has ridden far ahead, enjoying a race with some gentleman or another. I cannot be faulted for not being able to keep up. At Coughton we didn't ride often, and I never obtained the natural grace others possess.

Lost in my thoughts, I am suddenly aware of how quiet it is. Looking around me, it's clear I have fallen behind farther than I thought—or drifted too far off the path.

Just as I straighten in the saddle, the wind whips my new hat clean off my head, despite the pins that were supposed to hold it in place.

I make a grab for it, but it's too late and I wince as it lands with a plop in the stream.

Without thinking, I slide off the saddle. The hat is too precious to leave behind.

Doing everything I can, I discover I have no choice but to step into the stream to fetch the hat. It doesn't look deep. My riding gown will be soaked, but I am stubborn.

There's no one around that could help me now. I hitch up my gown and take a hesitant step. The water is colder than I expected. I feel it soaking into my boots. It's too late to turn back, so gritting my teeth, I continue. If I catch my death trying to retrieve this hat, I demand it to be burned at the stake. The sound of my laugh cuts through the silence of the air around me.

I am finally within reach of the hat and stop it from its trek farther down the stream.

I shake the weeds and algae off the hat as best as I

can. If nothing else, at least the silver buckle and ostrich feather are salvageable.

I turn to move back to the riverbank only to frown. My left foot has sunk into the mud. I pull with all my might only to lose my balance. With a splash, the cold water hits me. I am sputtering and struggle to right myself. My whole body is shaking from the shock.

I say a prayer thanking God that the water isn't deeper. I must be stupid to have thought this was a good idea.

The sound of cantering hooves fills the air. My horse snorts and paws the ground. A grey speckled horse is in front of me. He is a huge beast. I have to shade my eyes with my hand to see who the rider is. My breath hitches at seeing Raleigh there.

He leaps from the saddle.

"My lady, are you well?"

It's clear he intends to come rescue me. Mortification fills me.

"Stop," I say, holding up my hand. "I'm fine. No need to concern yourself."

He freezes mid-stride. Then he tilts his head, amused.

"Am I mistaken? I assumed this beast threw you from the saddle?" He regards my horse nearby.

"No, I thought today was the perfect day for a dip in the stream." My voice is biting with sarcasm. My teeth have begun chattering as the water seeps deeper into my clothes. I am hiding the hat behind my back, too embarrassed to have him discover that I would risk myself for something so small.

Raleigh's eyes soften. "My lady, you are cold. Let us save our arguments for later. You will catch your death if you remain in that stream."

I close my eyes, praying once more for strength, and set aside my pride. "My foot is stuck."

"The mud?" he guesses.

I nod.

Without waiting for more, he steps into the river, coming as close as he dares. He keeps his footing on the pebbles and darker ground, avoiding the silt and algae in the centre of the stream.

"Give me your hand," he says, bending forward with an outstretched hand.

I hesitate for a moment before reaching for it. The minute my hand is in his, he tightens his grip and pulls in one swift motion. As my leg comes free, I am unable to keep myself from bumping into his chest as the momentum carries me forward.

He grunts at the impact but only wraps his arms around me and pulls the both of us to shore.

"Are you hurt?"

I shake my head. "No. Just cold." Even though I was only in that stream for such a short time, my legs feel heavy. I want nothing more than to return to my rooms and order the maids to pile on the logs in the fireplace.

"Yes, I can see that. Your lips are going blue."

Finding the courage, I look up. His eyes are crinkled

in genuine concern. My heart is hammering in my chest at his closeness and the awkwardness of the situation.

My arms hang limply at my side. That darn hat has fallen to the ground.

"Allow me to take you back to court," he says, his words a soft caress.

"No," I say, shaking my head while finding the strength to step away from his warm embrace. "You cannot leave the queen."

"She has plenty of company. You, on the other hand..."

My eyes close as if they are trying to shut out my fear at being discovered alone with him.

"Exactly, my lord. How will this look if you take me back to the palace? As you have said, I am without company, but yourself and your—"

"My reputation precedes me?" He smirks. Then shakes his head. "The longer we argue over this the greater the chance you will become seriously ill. You can worry about your reputation after you've got out of these wet clothes. As soon as I have found someone who can look after you, I promise I shall leave you alone. I won't even dawdle or dare to inquire over your well-being."

"You are teasing me."

"And you are testing me." He takes a step forward, his expression losing any hint of amusement. "You can come willingly, or I can carry you off like the pirate you think I am. Your choice."

He's being far too serious and he's right. I'm being

foolish. "Thank you for your assistance. I appreciate the trouble you have gone through to help me."

"Very formal and proper. I doubt anyone could ever doubt you are not a saint."

Somehow his words strike me as an insult, but he whistles for his horse and it comes closer.

"I wonder if your horse will be able to keep up," he says as he reaches down to hand me my hat.

"It's borrowed," I start explaining, but then I find myself lifted up into the air and deposited on his saddle. He hands me his cloak with a challenging look that dares me to refuse. I avoid his gaze as he walks over to the gelding and leads him by the reins.

"Then I won't feel bad for calling him an old hag."

We are off without further comment. Raleigh keeps one hand gripped around my waist and I try to ignore the feel of his breath on the nape of my neck. He pushes the horses to go as fast as they can.

If he had made a fuss once we reached the stable yard and not merely escorted me to the door, then it would have cemented my embarrassment.

As it stands, I am whisked away inside while he presumably returns to the queen.

Blanche Parry, the queen's old nursemaid, is one of the few ladies who stayed behind. At nearly eighty years of age, she is the oldest woman I have ever met. She is half blind and sometimes flies into a temper, but none of us are fooled into thinking she has become simple-minded. When I enter the presence chamber, she stands and approaches me, her eyes squinting. I don't even get a word out before she places a hand on my cheek.

She clicks her tongue in disapproval.

"What happened to you?"

I open my mouth to respond, but she shakes her head. "Never mind. Let's see about getting you warmed up."

My clothes are removed and I am urged to sit by the fire, wrapped in thick furs. A maid comes with warm ale and I enjoy the warmth that spreads from my belly outward with every sip.

Later, one of the queen's doctors comes to examine me and gives me a packet of powders to drink with some wine to strengthen my constitution. I set little store by doctors and their potions, but I thank him and slip the brown paper into my pocket. All the while Blanche has been watching me from a seat by the window.

Now that the fuss has died down, she turns to me. "I hope this slip into the river wasn't because you were slipping away for some..." She can't bring herself to say it, but she waves her hands around as if to make her point.

A flush of heat warms my frozen cheeks.

"Nothing like that. My hat fell in the water. It was foolish of me."

She stares at me with a look of comprehension. Most here know of the poor state of my finances. So she says nothing more, besides coming over to give my hand one last comforting squeeze.

Perhaps it would've been better to let her go on thinking I had been meeting a lover in the woods.

CHAPTER 3

1585-1586

With my ear pressed to the door of the great hall, I listen for the cue to come in. Behind me, the other ladies are busy giggling and making last-minute adjustments to their costumes.

At last I hear the drums. I straighten up and nod to Catherine Howard, who with a snap of her fingers has everyone's attention. We line up. Just in time for the doors to be flung open.

I'm at the forefront of this group as we move between the arrangements of fauna in the great hall. Dressed in these light informal gowns, we move freely, spinning and twirling as the music dictates.

We are the sea, dressed in beautiful gowns covered in gauze stitched with pearls that catch the light and sparkle. On the cliffside is a water nymph waiting for her human love. Her father, King Neptune, wishes her to marry, but she doesn't like his choice. This water nymph, of course, is meant to represent our queen. She wears a long wig of reddish hair, and her virginal white gown mimics the gown the queen is wearing today.

The story takes a tragic turn as King Neptune sends his guards to capture her and bring her back to his watery kingdom.

We are meant to stand in their way but are captured. My gasp as strong arms wrap around my waist and twist me away is real. I nearly forgot myself.

"Shh. It's all right, Lady Bess," the familiar voice of Raleigh whispers in my ear. A trail of goose bumps travels down the side of my neck and I shudder.

"'Tis nothing but playacting," I say, but my voice comes out sounding breathless and no doubt has given me away.

We watch from the side-lines as the main guard throws a net, capturing the sea nymph. Just as he's about to drag her back into the sea, her human lover appears. The Earl of Southampton is dressed in a suit of gold cloth. Unlike the guards dressed in drab black, he is a burst of colour, green and gold, at his bosom a red rose.

A mock battle ensues between the guard and Southampton. Of course love prevails and he frees the nymph from her net.

They dance together, hands clasped on the stage, and disappear from the great hall before the end of the song.

We all break away and bow as the court applauds us. I can't help feeling distracted by Raleigh's presence hovering behind me. He remains near me, though his friends motion him over. Feeling flattered, I cannot stop the grin spreading across my face. We watch the queen for approval and find she is smiling lightly and clapping along. I cannot tell if she is pleased with it or not, but once Southampton is back she commends him for his beautiful footwork.

"It is a shame that I do not have a love waiting for me on a distant shore," she says, loud enough for everyone to hear despite her wistful tone.

Charles Blount, who was the creator of this little play, goes white. He jumps forward with a deep bow and then prostrates himself at her feet.

"It is the love of the people, not the love of a mere mortal, that I meant to represent. You have chosen us, the English people and land, to love and care for rather than..."

"I see." The queen's eyes are twinkling. "Then you have failed to get your message across." Her head tilts to the side. "Perhaps if your hero emerged from the bowels of the earth itself wearing the English flag."

She continues on in this vein for a while and then bursts out laughing. "Oh my, I have got ahead of myself. This was a wonderful piece of entertainment. I should be commending you, not giving you advice on how to fix it." The queen holds out her hand for him to kiss it and then invites him to sit beside her.

The Christmas season goes smoothly even though Leicester and Essex remain in the Netherlands. The queen is in a melancholic mood. She does her best not to show it, but she has neither taste for food nor desire for frivolity. She sequesters herself away with her council, going over plans and writing letters.

In March we know the war has swung the other way again. We enjoyed a few months of success and our men fought bravely. Sir Philip Sidney led his soldiers to victory at the battle of Armis and allowed our allies to retake the city. However, now the tide has turned. Even though the queen continues to send them money and supplies, they are intercepted by the Spanish fleet and cannot get through. All our hard-earned money goes instead into the Spanish coffers and the food into the bellies of the Spanish soldiers. We hope the wheat curdles in their stomachs and makes them sick.

I am working on some embroidery when Walter Raleigh and Sir Francis Drake come in. These two sea captains come dressed for business. They are a matched pair in the seriousness of their expressions. The queen is behind in her bedchamber, enjoying a private meal with her closest ladies, Catherine Howard among them.

I stand to stop them, though it is not my business to do so. Perhaps I simply wish to throw myself in his way again. I brush the thought away, focusing on the infamous Drake.

"My lords, the queen doesn't wish to be disturbed."

They stop in their tracks, sharing a look.

"That may be, my lady," Raleigh says. "But I am afraid we carry news that cannot wait."

I frown, but I straighten up as if to show I won't be easily pushed aside. "Her instructions were clear."

"I never knew the queen's ladies followed rules so closely." Drake's expression cracks. I imagine he's thinking of all the ladies he's managed to seduce. Famous sea captain or not, I reward him with my meanest glare.

"Stand down, friend," Raleigh says to him. "Can you not see this lioness is ready to bite your head off to protect her mistress from you?"

I blink. Memories flood back to me and I remember that childish promise I made to myself to be one.

Raleigh steps forward. "This is urgent. I understand why the queen might not wish to see us, but please..."

He is being genuine. I bite the inside of my cheeks before finally capitulating. "I shall step through to ask her."

"We shall wait," Raleigh says with a bow.

I catch the way Drake rolls his eyes but doesn't say anything to contradict me. I turn back to the closed oak door.

I realise I'm more frightened of interrupting the queen than I let on. Our relationship is new and rocky. With resolve to not let the men behind me sense my discomfort, I knock on the door gently and wait for an invitation.

Queen Elizabeth calls me in.

"Yes?"

"Drake and Raleigh are here to speak with you. They

say it cannot wait," I begin, but she interrupts me with a scoff.

"I distinctly remember holy oil anointing my fore-head." She taps her lip with a finger and looks at Blanche. "And something heavy placed on my head...but I can't recall..."

"A crown, Your Majesty," Blanche offers but then scolds her old charge. "Now don't be impertinent. She's just delivering the message to you, and you know men will be men. They never care about our time."

The queen reaches over and pats her hand. "I see I am never too old to be put in my place." Her expression falls as she sighs. In this moment her veneer of perfection falls away and she looks every bit her age.

I look away, embarrassed to have even thought this about her and fearful that she might be able to tell from my expression.

"Child, tell those two men out there that they will have to wait for me. I give you permission to bar the door by any means you deem necessary."

I bob a curtsy and retreat from the room.

Raleigh and Drake move away from Lady Hastings. Irritation fills me as I see they have been enjoying themselves while I have been facing the queen's censure.

"So?" Drake says, readjusting his jacket.

"I am afraid you shall have to wait for her majesty to finish."

Something flashes across his expression. I can only call it fury, but it is gone just as quickly as it appeared.

"This is important. We should have not stopped for you to…"

"Be calm," Raleigh says, but he keeps glancing over his shoulder in Lady Hastings's direction.

My irritation flares once more. I don't need his protection.

"Her majesty will see you when she is able to and not a moment sooner." I retreat back to my embroidery, keeping a scornful watch on the two men.

Raleigh has placed his hand on Drake's shoulder and is reassuring him. I hear him whisper, "You know how the queen can be. She doesn't like to be ordered around. If you want her to agree, you will go about this softly."

To my horror, he looks up and catches me watching. He gives me a wink before turning back to Drake.

At last Drake relents. With a nod and a sharp exhalation he marches to the chair by the fire, directly across from Lady Hastings. He looks like a different person as he leans forward with a sly smile to inquire about her day.

Such a flirt. I shake my head in disapproval as I nip the thread from the spool and focus on the work in front of me.

But I have forgotten about Raleigh. Only when his shadow blocks my light do I look up.

He's standing a few feet away from me, by no means crowding me, but it's becoming harder to breathe, as if the air has gone out of the room. I blame it on his electrifying presence. He's the sort of man who is used to commanding everyone's attention.

Defiantly, I press on with my work. My needle is stabbing in and out of the linen with increasing ferocity.

"We bother you so much?"

The question sounds so odd. He has spoken softly, as if he's coaxing a mare back into good behaviour. It only serves to further annoy me.

"The queen will be locked away for quite some time. So it seems as though we have time to get better acquainted. Tell me, how may we be forgiven?"

My thoughts remain as closed off to him as my expression of cool detachment.

He goes on, not caring I am so unresponsive, and begins pacing in front of me. "I've noticed you are very observant. Have you ever thought about taking up a position with Sir Walsingham? Or perhaps you already have."

Sir Francis Walsingham is the queen's spymaster. If this were any other day or moment, perhaps I would be flattered by the suggestion I would be a good spy. But instead I am irked by his condescending tone. I reach into my basket for another colour, but the spool slips from my grip and rolls on the ground until it is stopped by Raleigh's boot.

He bends at the waist and retrieves it with the grace of a dancer. Instinctually, I reach out for it. His hand clasps mine, the spool trapped between us. Our eyes lock on each other. At last he has succeeded in capturing my attention.

Having never been so close to him before, I begin a close study of his features: from his full crooked lips to those mesmerising eyes. I note the flecks of yellow among the green. Savouring the delicious feeling of his hand on mine, I find myself leaning toward him rather than away. My expression turns grim as I try and fail to recall why I was angry with him in the first place.

"I repulse you so much?"

He lets go of my hand and steps away.

"No." Slowly, logic overcomes the unmistakable growing desire. There's a fresh burst of pleasure when I see he is determined to remain by my side.

By the time I have steadied myself enough to speak, the needle is rethreaded and I begin my work anew. "I just don't appreciate jokes made at my expense."

From the corner of my eye I see the frown on his face deepen. "I meant no insult, my lady."

I shrug. "Then you should learn to choose your words more carefully." I look him straight in the eye. "And your manners—you have forgotten to wear your gloves in the presence of her majesty."

His tense expression is replaced with a coy grin, and he places a hand over his heart. "Indeed. It is unimaginable that I should come before her majesty so...naked."

I tremble at the improper word and glance around to see if anyone has heard.

He changes tack. "Perhaps it speaks to the urgency of the matter that brings me here seeking an audience. One that you prevented."

I shake my head. "It was her wish not to be disturbed."

He shrugs. "But if you hadn't stood in our way, then

we could have surprised her and claimed we were ignorant of her wishes."

The needle slips from my grasp and I pierce the linen in the wrong place. So he and Drake had planned this all along? Well, I refuse to feel bad for thwarting them.

As I rush to correct my mistake, he leans forward, pressing on. "It is admirable how loyal you are to your mistress. I commend you for that—and your many other qualities."

My cheeks heat at his words, something I pray he doesn't notice as I keep my gaze glued to my work. This might all be a game to him, but clearly my heart doesn't know the difference and is now hammering away in my chest.

"I swear I shall strive to earn your good opinion. It is my desire that we become good friends and put aside our differences."

I don't know which terrifies me more. I swallow down the bubbling fear and desire while glancing toward the oak door, wondering how much longer the queen will keep these men waiting. If it is her wish to make a point, then she will prolong her lunch indefinitely, and thus my torment.

"I must confess something else, my lady."

This interrupts my inner turmoil. "Yes?"

"I did inquire after your well-being after your dip in the river. So I was not true to my word."

"I never expected you to be," I say. This is altogether too blunt for courtly speech, but I refuse to back down.

"See," he says. "You continue to show how wise you truly are. Men are fickle things."

"I've often heard the same thing said about women."

"We are all creatures cut from the same cloth." He laughs, and that pearl dangling from his left ear shakes with him. He catches me staring at it and flicks it absent-mindedly. "I see you've noticed my most prized possession."

As if such a huge pearl would be easy to miss, but curiosity gets the better of me and I cannot stop myself from speaking. "I heard you sailed to the New World and stole it from the tomb of Cortez."

His gleaming eyes tell me I've played right into his hands. He leans forward ever so slightly and I catch a whiff of his masculine scent. "You seem to know a lot about me."

This time I don't take the bait. To my dismay, it merely encourages him.

"Would you like to become even better acquainted? At this very moment?"

He is a silver-tongued devil. Even as I turn my most hateful glare on him, I can see he is amused. He enjoys playing this game of cat and mouse. The thought settles the unsettling feeling growing in the pit of my stomach. This is all a bit of fun. Nothing more.

"I would like to know where that pearl came from." Inwardly, I congratulate myself on my composure.

The corners of his lips twitch as if he's fighting back a smile. "I'll tell you a secret. One I've told no one before..."

How many other women has he said the exact same thing to before? But I wait patiently to hear his tale.

"The first ship I ever raided for her majesty carried treasure from the New World. I came upon the horde alone and couldn't contain my glee—"

"A dragon." I bite my lower lip. I didn't mean to interrupt.

"Flattering you should think of me as one."

My lips purse. That was certainly not a compliment, but I say nothing more.

"What should happen at that very moment but a shot comes whizzing by my ear." He points to his pierced ear. "It missed me by the width of a hair. The captain had not been content to let us have his treasure without a fight. I still carry the scar."

I can see how he expects this to play out. The lingering pauses, the lilt in his voice. He's a poet as well. But Raleigh will find I am not so easily entranced. "I'd be surprised if a sailor such as yourself didn't have a great many scars," I say rather flippantly. At the surprised look on his face I carry on against my better judgment. "But they aren't special. Even I carry a few of my own."

Verbal sparring has never been my strong suit. I never know when to stop, and now I have provided him with the perfect opening.

By a stroke of luck, we hear the latch on the oak door open. I expect Raleigh to leave right away, but instead he captures my hand again, placing a delicate kiss on the back of my hand. "I look forward to one day discovering all of them," he whispers so low and fast I think I imagined it.

Before I have even begun to process what he said, he's waiting in the centre of the room. Drake is at his side. When I study his features, there is no sign of what transpired between us. Then again, for a man like Raleigh flirting must be a daily occurrence. I am rather snide as I equate his desire to flirt with his need for air, and just like breathing he does it without thinking. As if he can't help himself. A part of me is envious how he can push down emotions so easily.

The queen appears, her face regal and annoyed, but she allows the two men to come forward and pay her homage. Once they have grovelled enough, she hears them out.

Their words help me find my centre. There are more important issues at hand than the feel of his lips on my skin and the emotions they awakened.

"With your permission, Your Majesty, I want to take my ships to raid the Spanish coast and then travel north to break the blockade so we can restore our access to the Netherlands."

"I do not know if I can countenance such a venture."

"Your Majesty." Drake steps forward, his dark eyes downcast. "Far be it from me to disagree with you, but you are far too lenient with the Spanish—"

"We are defending our allies, but to engage with them on the open sea in this way would be just the invitation they need to invade our shores."

"I beg your pardon, my queen, but they already have

a reason. Your cousin remains in your keeping. By your mercy she is still alive to be used by the Catholics and Spanish alike who wish to usurp your throne."

A hush falls over the room at his words. Several people turn toward me to gauge my reaction. My whole body tenses and my ears are ringing with embarrassment. For once I find solace in playing the part of a meek lady with her eyes demurely cast down. I am one of the only ladies at court that is openly Catholic. Everyone expects me to go the way of my aunt, who conspired on Mary Stuart's behalf.

She lost her head while the queen's cousin managed to survive. Why the queen extended such mercy is unclear. The Tudors have never balked at the prospect of killing their kin before. What makes Mary Stuart different? That is a question that has plagued Queen Elizabeth's councillors for years. Yet even after all this time, they have failed to unravel the mystery.

I didn't know my aunt very well, nor did I weep to hear of her execution, but I did feel the pang of injustice keenly. If my aunt was guilty, so was the Scots queen. Many of her supporters died on her behalf, including the Duke of Norfolk. Should her punishment not be the same?

If this were a fable, the moral would be that justice is an illusion. My thumb runs over the embroidered deer with its speckled coat. Now I wish I had picked a different motif to work on. I can imagine the fear it must feel being chased by baying hounds. I will rethink my work once their attention is diverted.

"My cousin has nothing to do with this. She will pay for her crimes in due course. We all have to answer to God one day, and I prefer to do so with a clean conscience." The queen speaks with such finality that it takes all the men's courage not to take a step back.

Then her expression softens. "I long for a walk in the gardens. The pair of you may join me and we may discuss your plans."

A few ladies step forward, eager to be invited on this jaunt, but I shrink farther back into my seat, hoping to be left to my own devices in the presence chamber.

A few days later we are preparing to ride out on a hunt to enjoy the fresh spring air. I find a note tucked into the pommel of my saddle. I tuck it into the sleeve of my gown without a second glance.

Secret notes always seem to find me at the most inopportune moments.

In the beginning I found them exciting and curiosity would get the better of me and I would read them before handing them over. But there's only so often you can read the same thing over and over again.

Cecil was right when he placed me in the queen's household that many would try to use me to garner information about the queen or involve me in Catholic conspiracies.

I know which hand feeds me, and I am not so devout that I would betray my own interests. I do as I am bid by my betters and inform them of any whiff of scandal and plots that come my way. It's a lucrative business and far safer than intriguing.

After we return, exhausted from our ride, I try to find the opportunity to slip away, but I am foiled at every turn. Normally I wouldn't resent these banal tasks that keep me running from one end of the castle to the other, but today I find myself itching for freedom. When the queen announces she will dine in private today, I know this will be my chance. After her meal we will have to begin to get her ready for the evening. Even after she changes into her robes, she will not go to bed right away, as she prefers to stay up late working or translating works to keep her mind sharp. She is proud of her knowledge of language and her intellect. I would treasure and cultivate it just as she does if I were in her position. Her strong like and admiration for the topic is likely fuelled by her fear of advancing years. She often pretends that it doesn't bother her, that she is still as spry as she was in her youth, but she also fears the complicity that comes with age, the dullness that settles in and spreads like a virus over one until she finds herself hunched over and unable to do much else besides sleep and eat.

I make my excuses and slip out of the queen's presence chamber. I make my way to the great hall and search among the crowd for Arthur's familiar face.

The queen being absent means that decorum has slipped. Not enough for the great hall to have become no better than a tavern hall, but enough to make it difficult for me with my wide gown to make my way over to him.

The only boon of the situation is that at the very least I can be concealed in the chaos.

As I cross the room, my eyes catch the glittering plates set before the queen's seat. Even though she isn't here, servants still serve the high table. It is a signal of her wealth and opulence. A royal tradition maintained for generations. At least I know the cold food will be given to the kitchen staff or the hungry souls waiting outside the palace gates. The court produces a massive amount of waste. As someone who helps oversee the servants preparing baskets of food for the destitute, I have seen exactly how much food we nobles discard.

I slide into the vacant seat beside my brother with as much grace as the situation allows.

Arthur is pleased to see me. "It has been too long, sister." His courtier's smile is replaced with a genuine one.

"You as well. I hope you have been keeping yourself out of trouble," I say, looking over at the men playing cards nearby.

"You know I am far too responsible for gambling. Besides, there are better ventures to occupy myself with."

"Oh?"

"Our mother's marriage."

I pull away in shock. "What!"

"Shhh. Keep your voice down."

I lean closer to him so we cannot be overheard. "Tell me you are jesting."

"I assure you I am not." He picks up a jug of ale and pours himself a generous helping. "Her letter arrived to me this morning. I haven't had a chance to speak to you."

"Who?" I find it so hard to imagine who might have enticed my pious mother away from her black. Who would want her? I close my eyes in fear that some fortune hunter has got his claws into her. Not that she has a fortune, but her family name is worth something still.

"Adrian Stokes."

My frown only deepens. "He's a widower twice over. What business does he have with our mother?"

"What, indeed," Arthur mutters into his goblet.

I give my head a little shake. "This isn't the discussion I came to have. Here." Without turning toward him, I slide the sealed letter into his hands underneath the table. His hand wraps around it. For a moment I suspect he wishes to crumple it and rip it to shreds, but instead he tucks it away into the purse at his waist.

"I'll take care of this first thing in the morning." His mood has taken a shift for the worse.

Nudging his elbow, I take it upon myself to refill his cup. "Should we be concerned about our mother? There's nothing we can do, and maybe she's truly found happiness with him."

His face turns a subtle shade of green to match his jacket. I laugh, knowing how put off he is by the thought of our mother with a lover. While we often agree, my brother clearly has other ideas about how our elderly mother should be spending her time. By contrast, the thought of her giving up the pretence of being a sombre woman thrills me.

"I cannot comment on that, but he hardly has much to gain from marrying her—" He clears his throat. "I met him once before. He doesn't seem like the tyrannical sort of man that might cause trouble for her."

"Good." Watching him struggle over his words makes me struggle to hold back my smile. My poor brother. I must save him. "Then, as shocking as this is, we will have to congratulate her and do so earnestly. But what of your plans? Has a date been set yet?"

His marriage to Lady Ann Lucas has been postponed once already. Her father keeps faltering and trying to make changes to the contract. It is tragic that matters can't be hurried along. The two of them are so madly in love with each other that I'm shocked they haven't eloped yet. To make matters worse, Ann's father has taken her away from court—perhaps to ensure that matters between them don't go too far making a marriage necessary.

"I hope to beat our mother to the altar at least," he says, his tone as bitter as the ale he is drinking.

"I am sure she will agree to those terms." I cannot help but chuckle. "Brother, jealousy does not become you. I hope you too shall be happy and settled. Too many worries plague you."

My hand is on his shoulder. He looks up at me, his expression lighter, and says, "At least you are here to listen to my concerns. I appreciate it."

"I'm glad you noticed. Now I must be off."

"Jumping back into the fray?"

A chuckle escapes me. "Something like that."

My brother gets his wish. In the summer he finally weds Lady Ann, and I travel to Coughton Court to see them installed as lord and lady.

The reunion with my mother is more awkward. She takes a break from Adrian Stokes to approach me. For once she is bashful, and as I kneel for her blessing she greets me warmly.

"It has been far too long since I have seen you. Court agrees with you," she says, patting my cheek. "You have blossomed into a beautiful young woman."

When I was younger, a comment like that would have made me blush. Truly court must have hardened my heart if I can hear her say that and not even blink.

"And yourself? Arthur tells me you plan to marry again."

My mother turns beet red. "It is true, though we shall wait for the autumn. Arthur is installing us in a little house not far from here. I am grateful for his care of me."

My court training keeps my expression from shifting. I would have expected her to be furious to be sent away from Coughton, though perhaps she doesn't want her new marriage to begin where her old one ended. "I am so glad that you have found happiness." Taking her hands in my own I say, "truly."

She gives me a smile that warms my heart. "Thank you. It has been difficult for me. After your father died, I had so many worries thrust upon my shoulders. I wanted nothing more than to do my duty by all of you. Now that most of you are grown, I find I can allow myself to think of myself. Perhaps I am selfish..." Her voice becomes small as she trails off. I am taken aback to see this indomitable spirit from my childhood reduced to this.

For the first time I realise I stand a head taller and am more finely dressed than she is. In many ways she's still my mother, but at this exact moment, our roles are reversed: she wants my permission to marry Adrian Stokes. My eyes snap to him talking to someone off in the distance. I catch how he keeps gazing our way, a look of concern flitting across his face.

When I look back at my mother, I smile. "There is nothing wrong with wanting a new adventure," I say, hoping that my reassurance counteracts anything my brother might have said. "Mother, you cannot know how much I wish to see you happy. Everyone deserves joy in their life. If you want to marry him, I could never gainsay you."

Her palm caresses my cheek, and her eyes glisten with unshed tears. Life has not been easy for my mother. My brother and I were often the cause of many of her difficulties. Perhaps we were wrong, but at least I can lend her my support in this.

Then she clears her throat and retreats behind her courtly mask. We re-join our guests while I do my best to avoid my brother's searching gaze.

My time away from her majesty's side is short. Being a lady-in-waiting means dedicating your life to her. Many haven't left the court in years. In a way I am lucky that I am not one of her treasured few companions that she cannot live without.

Despite my best attempt to slip back into her rooms unnoticed, she singles me out. At a motion from her I step forward and bow three times.

"Tell me who was in attendance at your brother's wedding? It had been delayed several times already, if I recall correctly," the queen says. "I hope Lady Ann is happily settled into her new home."

Not wishing to jump into any particulars, I curtsy and keep my answers brief. "As always, you are correct, Your Majesty. On both accounts."

The gleam of pleasure is back in her eye, but she doesn't hesitate to scold me. "Lady Bess, you weren't here to select the costumes for the play put on a fortnight ago, and it showed."

My skin burns with the heat of the compliment and the embarrassment that follows. "I shall not be remiss in my duties again."

Her dark eyes, inherited from her Boleyn mother, snap up at that. "I would hope not."

I curtsy low and eagerly disappear among the throng of courtiers. Eager for anonymity, I am shocked when a hand finds its way in mine. It takes all my willpower not to flinch or pull away. Slowly, I turn to see it is Raleigh who has captured me. Yet again.

My eyebrow shoots up in question.

"You were sorely missed. The queen does not tease you, if that is what you feared."

The air in my lungs escapes with a little gasp. "I fear nothing." The quick retort of a child. Collecting myself, I soften my tone to a whisper, aware of people looking our way. "But are you confessing to having missed me? I had no idea you even noticed me."

He doesn't answer, which terrifies me more. I remember him saying that he wishes we were better acquainted. The longer those green eyes are on me the weaker I feel. Thankfully, he breaks off studying me with a slight bow of his head and releases my hand. As I continue on my way, I wonder what game he is playing with me and why the thought of another conversation makes me ache with anticipation.

In autumn, a messenger arrives from Leicester in the Netherlands. We watch him bow to the queen and hesitate at her instruction to rise. He has not requested a private audience, but we can see that the news is bad.

The great hall is packed with people, so whatever is about to be said has been carefully prepared to invoke the desired response.

"Tell me, what brings you rushing into my court with an inch of mud on your cloak?" The queen's voice echoes around the room.

"Your Majesty, I bring you sad tidings." The messenger's voice trembles and I can see he wishes to be away from the court. He is not a willing actor, but this adds to his charm.

"Tell me then and be swift. The longer you prolong

this, the longer I suffer from anticipation." The queen is direct but soothing in her delivery.

With another hard swallow that even I from this great distance can see, he begins his tale.

"On October seventeenth your loyal commander and soldier died of wounds he sustained in the Battle of Zutphen—" He falters. "Your Majesty, I bring you grievous tidings that Sir Philip Sidney is dead." A collective sharp intake of breath from the gathered people interrupts him.

From the corner of my eye I see the willowy figure of Sir Walsingham disappear through a doorway. Sidney is —was his son-in-law. As the spymaster for the queen, he must have known already, but perhaps now that the news is confirmed publicly he is finally allowed to grieve.

"He prayed for Your Majesty to his last breath." The messenger goes on in this vein for a while. He recalls all of Sidney's great deeds and his bravery on the field of battle.

A tear escapes from the queen's eye and leaves a streak in the queen's white lead mask as it travels down. Her hand touching her throat shakes as she struggles to compose herself.

When the messenger is done, she stands to address us all. "He shall be brought back to England to be given a hero's burial. It's the very least he deserves. A true knight like him will never be forgotten. We shall ensure his death is not in vain and will prevail over our enemies."

We all murmur in agreement.

Just as we all wish prayers were enough to ensure

victory over the Spanish. Success seems to be creeping farther out of reach with each passing month.

I bow my head and say a private prayer for the safety of my brothers. Should the war continue, they will be called to serve the country, and I cannot bear the thought of losing them in war.

CHAPTER 4

1586 - 1587

"Where's the prayer book from Duke D'Orleans? I shall wear it tonight." The queen is surrounded by her gentlewomen. We dart around her like busy bees. Someone files her nails while another arranges the pleats of her dress.

I'm on the outskirts, so I step forward and volunteer to fetch it myself. Catherine Howard places the keys to the storerooms in my hands and off I fly down the familiar passageways and corridors. Only when I come to a dimly lit gallery does my pace slow. There's also the matter of the gentleman pacing at the other end of the hall.

He's failed to notice me. His focus is so intent on the piece of paper in his hand, muttering underneath his breath. I cannot help but study his handsome profile. Walter Raleigh hides himself behind his guarded confidence. This is the first time I have seen what lies beyond the mask. His brows are scrunched in concentration, and there's a sense of wariness in his posture.

I feel guilty for having spied on him for so long, so I clear my throat. He jolts out of his thoughts and looks up at me with a glare, which disappears once he sees me.

My heart races at seeing how his expression had softened.

"Lady Bess, I hardly expected you to be here." He looks out the window as if the night sky will tell him the time. "Has supper already begun?"

"Nearly," I say. "I am on an errand for the queen." I step forward, though it would be wiser for me to turn tail and flee the other way.

"How is she this evening?"

"Sir, you know how precious information is," I say. It's not a lie. Many of the queen's councillors bribe her gentlewomen on a daily basis for such information.

"What is your fee?" He takes a step forward and the candlelight casts his face in shadow, but I can see the sincerity in his expression has not gone away, though I believe I catch a hint of amusement in his tone.

I tap a finger to my cheek as if I am deep in thought. "That would be difficult to determine. Usually a shilling would be enough, but this time I might exchange information for information."

Step by step he has been approaching. By the time I finish he's within arm's reach. Overcome by his closeness, my senses are heightened and alert to his every move. A growing eagerness and excitement spreads from the pit of my belly outward.

He takes another step forward, and his hand reaches out to me. I should step away, but I'm dizzy with emotion and my eyes begin to close instead. He tilts my chin upward, forcing me to meet his intense gaze. "What information would you wish from me?" His thumb grazes my lower lip, sending a fresh wave of goose bumps over my skin.

The spell he has cast over me holds me in place. Defiant, I tell myself I am simply refusing to let him see how his actions affect me. I swear I am indifferent to him.

"What has you creeping about in dark corridors at this time of evening?" I say, my eyes travelling down to the paper he holds in his free hand. "More specifically, I wish to know what is written on that piece of paper."

Does he know how shocked I feel at my own words? He lets nothing slip as he takes a deep breath. I watch the swell of his chest as he does so, feeling that time has frozen and I am trapped in this personal hell of my own making.

"Shall I read it to you, Elizabeth?"

I flush at the use of my name in such a familiar way.

He doesn't wait for my answer, but he steps away to read aloud.

"To praise thy life or wail thy worthy death,
And want thy wit—thy wit high,
pure, divine—
Is far beyond the power of mortal line,
Nor any one hath worth that draweth breath..."

It's a beautiful poem. By the end of it I feel the sting of tears in the corner of my eyes. The tension in the room is replaced by general melancholia. I want nothing more than to reach out and soothe him.

"For Sir Philip?"

A firm nod confirms my suspicions. "You do him a great honour with your words. The queen will be—" It is hard to find the right word. "She will be pleased with it."

A sardonic smile spreads across his face. "Enough to throw a penny my way, like every other common minstrel."

"You deserve far more than that. And you are far from common." I tilt my head, considering him. "But you know that and you are merely seeking a compliment."

His laugh is low but reveals I have caught him. "I am guilty as charged."

"To fulfil my end of the bargain, I will tell you that the queen is in high spirits. I assume the news from the Netherlands is good and France has pledged to assist us against the Spanish. I don't know how she will take the poem if you plan on presenting it to her tonight."

He thinks for a moment. "I shall hold on to this for the right moment. Her majesty deserves a night of joy and frivolity."

"The state funeral is to be held in a few weeks. The moment might come..." I begin to say before trailing off, hating that I volunteered the information so freely and without guile.

"Thank you for informing me, Lady Bess." He steps forward. My body freezes at his approach. His affect upon me is unnatural. Before I know it, he places a kiss on my cheek. There is nothing romantic about the gesture. It is one I have often seen and performed myself. Yet my eyes close and I breathe in his scent, wishing he would linger a moment longer.

"You must not let me keep you," he says, but there's an unmistakable tantalising invitation behind his words.

"You must excuse me." I curtsy and flee down the gallery, not daring to look back. All the while I curse myself for being such a fool.

The queen's good mood is cut short by the pressure from parliament for her to act. The shadow of the Queen of Scots has hung over us all. She was found guilty at the trial the summer before, yet the queen in her mercy allowed her to live.

I am there in her privy chamber, helping to pack away the jewellery she wore to Mass, when I hear raised voices outside her door. The queen, seeing my concern, gives me a wiry smile.

"Don't fret, Lady Bess," she says with a heavy sigh. "I know what is about to come storming through that door."

I leap out in front of her as if I'm about to step in front of an assassin. My actions cause a stir and I am embarrassed.

"If you do not wish to admit them, then I will barricade the door myself," I say with as much stoicism as I can manage.

"Really, Lady Bess?" She shakes her head. "That would be unbecoming of a young lady such as yourself.

Though I appreciate the sentiment, I should allow the thorn to be pulled from my side."

I am confused, so she clarifies. "At the heart of every problem a person faces two options. The first is to ignore it and let it fester. Perhaps it will heal on its own. But take it from an old woman with much more experience: it rarely does. So that leaves you with the second option which is to yank it out as fast as possible. It will hurt. Yet, it will be over quick."

"But you are the queen. You can simply order the problem to go away."

She laughs at my jest. "I wish it were that easy. But I shall make an addendum to my prayers tonight. Perhaps God will answer me this time."

In years to come I will return to this conversation over and over again.

Six days later, I am helping to clean up after an evening of card playing. The queen has forbidden gambling beyond playing for chips. It is these marble chips that I am making sure are swept into their boxes to be laid aside for another day when I hear the creak of a door, followed by hurried whispers. Carefully, I set down the box I am holding and approach one of the many doors in and out of the queen's privy chamber.

Each of her rooms has multiple entrances and secret passageways. In times of war they were used as safe passages for the household to escape. Now...

I wonder if I should cry out. If this is an assassin or some terrible plot against the queen, I need to alert the guards, but intuition tells me that no assassin would be whispering in a gallery so close to their quarry.

I pull back the tapestry to expose a door hidden behind it. As carefully as I can I push it open just in time to see Richard Rich in the dimly lit hallway bowing to a figure hidden by shadows before he goes racing back the way he came.

A hand covers my mouth and a voice whispers in my ear, "Don't cry out."

I relax only when my mind realises that it is Catherine Howard. She releases me the second she feels me relax in her grip.

"Since you've been a nosy little mouse, follow him."

"What?"

"Follow him to the courtyard and report back what he does. Now."

My eyes are wide as I try to process what she is saying. She gives me a little shove and I turn to obey.

The shadow he had been talking to is gone, so I rush down the stairs in the direction Richard Rich took. Am I going quietly enough? My silk slippers don't echo down the stairwell as his heeled boots do, but the fabric of my dress rustles with each move. I cannot be certain, but I pray God mutes my steps. Though if he confronted me, I wouldn't even know why I am following him in the dead of night.

My heart pounding, I dare not breathe as I follow him from the main building to the stables beyond. I watch him slip onto a horse and ride out in the middle of the night. His destination? I could never guess.

I return the way I came, mulling over what I saw.

Catherine Howard waits for me in the queen's privy chamber, her eyebrow arched.

"He got on a horse and left."

"Did anyone approach him? Did he speak to anyone else?"

Shaking my head, I relax at last to see her tense expression drop. She smiles at me and nods.

"Good. This stays between us. Mention this to no one."

"I swear I won't."

She gives a little shrug of her shoulders as though she doesn't care either way. "What would you have to report anyway? And then we would know if you can be trusted or not. There would be no winning for you."

I move past her, biting my tongue to keep myself from making a scathing retort. Once I retire to my bed, I think to myself that she has underestimated me. This information would fetch a high price. What was he up to though? What mission did the queen send him on? Or perhaps he was delivering her news? It doesn't concern me overly much. My loyalties lie firmly with the queen. For now I am certain she was the one hidden in the shadows or another of her minions doing her bidding.

By morning I have trained myself to forget I ever saw anything. When Lady Holland comments on the dark circles under my eyes, I claim to have had an upset stomach.

"I can get you a tincture," she says underneath her

breath. "There's a physician who does wonders for me at times like these."

I shake my head. "I am better already. After another night of proper sleep I shall recover fully."

"You better pray we get to rest." She nods her head toward the queen. "The council wishes to speak to her this morning about an urgent matter."

My interest is piqued. "Do you know about what?"

Lady Holland fiddles with the ruby ring on her finger. "No idea."

Inwardly, I roll my eyes. I am tempted, but the information is not worth parting with a few coins.

Six days later, when a messenger brings news of Mary, Queen of Scots' execution, I have my answers. The pieces of the puzzle fit neatly together and I can see everything so clearly.

As I fight to school my features, the queen is busy working herself up into a fit of rage and despair. She pulls at her hair, and tears stream down her cheeks as she orders the arrest of the messenger and her councillors to report to her. It's beautifully performed, but I can only watch it from behind a misty haze.

It's true she signed the death warrant a few days ago, but she didn't give any explicit instructions for it to be carried out.

At least that is the official story the queen is keen on spreading. Even if no one believes her, very few have proof to contradict her. Richard Rich is imprisoned in the tower and everyone expects him to be executed. He is declared a traitor and loses his seat in parliament. Pointedly, no official trial is held and the queen never signs an attainder against him. Some may shrug this off and say she is forgetful or emotional. However, one look at him when he is brought in front of her to be berated tells me that he doesn't fear the scaffold. He might beg the queen for mercy, but he is far too steady on his feet and his delivery is missing the gravitas needed for such a situation.

"You overreached yourself, sir," the queen condemns him. Her eyes narrow into slits. "Like many others of my council, you sought to force my hand in this."

"Your Majes—"

She cuts him off. "You men are all the same, thinking you know better than me. But I tell you and all those in this room, it is I, Elizabeth, who rules."

I catch more than a few men take a step back at the venomous words, and others go pale.

In the coming days, very few think of the poor woman who now lies dead. Many are relieved. Others worry about the reaction in Europe as the news spreads. Even the queen's carefully managed story will not be enough to suppress Spain's reaction. Then there are those closer to home who would have used Mary as their pawn. They do not shed too many tears before beginning to search for another Catholic heir to put on the English throne. So I try to force myself to think of Mary and what it must have been like to be imprisoned with the threat of death hanging over her for over twenty years? Did she feel relief when it was all over?

We will go to war over her grave.

We will go on using her as a pawn in this twisted game of power.

Shame on us all.

The February wind cuts through the layers of furs and coats and leaves me shivering. My cheeks have no protection as we stand watching the funeral procession from the parapets. By now they have gone numb. I make a note to ask Lady Holland for a salve to put on my skin tonight. The last thing I want is the pain of cracked skin. While I do my best to shield myself from every gust of wind, ahead of me our queen is a statue of marble. Nothing can make her falter—and if something could, it certainly wouldn't be something as mundane as the weather. I often wish I had an inch of her resolve.

We hear the drums and the slow stamp of feet as the coffin is borne forward through the crowded streets of London. Sir Francis Walsingham has spared no expense on this stately funeral. The queen herself would be hard pressed to command one as grand as this. No less than eight horses, whose matching black coats reflect the sun, draw the litter carrying the coffin. The litter itself is decorated sumptuously in rich velvets. Behind it come the men. I can make out Leicester, who stands as the primary mourner leading the way. Women do not attend the funerals of men, but the queen has decided to honour England's hero with this appearance. She is using Sidney's funeral to make people forget about the Queen of Scots. His death has been a blow to the troops' morale, but she is seeking to capitalise on it.

Soon the legends that spring forth will eclipse the real man.

We need legends now more than ever. This grand ceremony, with the queen in deepest black and the court in full mourning, is a public relations exercise. Sir Philip Sidney's memory will be enshrined in the hearts of all loyal Englishmen, and they will strive to achieve even half of his accomplishments—regardless of how exaggerated they might be.

My mind is unable to focus on the departed. Instead, my eyes search the procession for Raleigh. A glint of white among the sea of black catches my eye, but it is not him but rather the silver button of some other gentleman.

I scold myself for my ridiculousness.

"Are you well?" Lady Alice asks under her breath.

I nod. "The cold." Indeed I notice her lips are tinged with blue.

She looks sympathetic but can offer me no respite besides an encouraging smile.

The queen dines in private with her favoured few. Among them is Leicester, whose pale pallor indicates an illness beyond the sadness over the loss of his close friend and relative. Those of us not invited to dine with her are relegated to dinner in the great hall.

There is no boisterous conversation or music. We are sombre as we pick at our food.

It's hard to imagine spring in the depths of winter. This feeling of being trapped is not unusual, but the more I look around me the more I am certain I have missed something. This is more than just the weather or the loss of a dear companion. We've known about Sidney's death for months. Yet the faces in the great hall are withdrawn as if they have just been told. Those who would know more are tucked away with the queen.

I bite my lower lip. Without thinking, my eyes travel to the table at the back of the great hall where my brother would normally be found. But Arthur has taken up his duties in the country and is overseeing the stewardship of his lands. He won't be back until parliament is called to sit again—knowing the queen and her dislike for assembling parliament, this will take quite some time.

A wave of loneliness and isolation threatens to overwhelm me. It doesn't make sense. I am surrounded by hundreds of people and, arguably, I am kept very busy. So why now?

Wanting some fresh air, I get to my feet and slip away. I am ready to cry and I have no idea what could possibly have made me so emotional.

I stand before a window looking out at the sky painted in purples and red by the setting sun. Someone behind me clears his throat. Almost at once I know who it is. The tell-tale pounding of my heart is a clear indication.

"Good evening," I say, not wishing to be impolite, but I don't want to appear desperate either.

He comes to stand beside me, yet he keeps a respectable distance. "It's a beautiful evening. Yet I find you here looking as though you are about to cry, and I cannot help myself from wondering why."

"Why should it surprise you that I am about to cry? Is the world not a horrible place worth shedding my tears over?"

"I would not have you think of the world as such. You deserve to feel nothing but joy."

I tilt my head at the sentiment. It's an empty wish and I feel no shame telling him so. "If I felt no pain or sadness, I could never appreciate or understand the joy."

He chuckles. "See. Such seriousness does not belong in such a young person."

"You talk as if you are my elder." Somehow I cannot bear the thought that he sees me as some young immature woman he must coddle.

"I have some years on you. But I speak more of my experience in life. I have seen too much."

"Now who is being dramatic?"

"Touché." He turns to face me. "I am happy to have made you smile though."

A wave of embarrassment sweeps over me, wiping away the remnants of the smile I hadn't even realised was there.

"Why do you always flinch away like this?"

He is genuinely perplexed by my reaction to him. If only he knew that I am just as confused. The culprit is likely my lack of control and composure around him, but how can I voice that? I can barely admit it to myself.

"I am not flinching. Or at least it's not my intention. I distrust your interest in me." I cannot believe I am speaking so frankly, but this seems to have been the right thing to say.

"Are you usually so shy? I have watched you and you don't seem to be a shy woman by nature. So what is it about me that puts you so on edge?"

Clouds obscure the last remaining sunlight, casting him into darkness. Though Raleigh towers over most men at court, he has a lanky build rather than being wide in the shoulders. Other men might have concealed this by wearing padded shoulders, even cropping their hair short to keep the effeminate curls at bay. However, his confidence and his direct gaze create quite an alluring illusion. Again, my eyes are drawn to the pearl hanging from his ear. In this dim light, realisation dawns on me.

"You lied to me."

I cannot see his expression, but I imagine his eyebrow is raised. "What?"

"You once told me you wear the pearl to remind you of your adventures, but looking at you now, I think you had something else entirely in mind."

He is quiet, an invitation to continue.

"You are the very image of the queen, yet male. Your style and grace, the pearl which happens to be her favourite gem, and your hair—all a mirror of her."

He lifts his hands and claps lightly. The sound makes me shiver.

"Well done, milady." He inclines his head. "I could deny it, but I am not ashamed. I am proud to copy our queen. She calls me her pug and I shall let her dress me as she pleases, for all things good about me belong to her."

"Your motto." I nod, recalling the Latin: *amor et virtus*. "Would loyalty not suit your purposes better? It wouldn't be too late to change it."

"It would be too on the nose. Loyalty is easy to give. I don't wish to be seen as some dog. However, I want to make everyone understand that I hold myself to the highest standards. Besides, I would not want it to be said I was ever disingenuous."

"Why would you be disingenuous?"

"One's loyalty is doled out to many recipients, and I expect that one day it will be divided further still," he says, his voice rough around the edges. "The queen has my virtue, for all that is good in me is hers. Loyalty is part of a larger piece of what I can offer her."

Above all else I want to learn more, but I hold myself back from pressing him. "I hadn't considered it that way," I say, though it pains me I have spoken so naively. "What else can you offer her then? How is love different from virtue?"

The clouds have moved on and light seems to flood the window. He is smiling at me in that gentle way of his. "I hadn't known you were in the mood for a debate this evening."

"To be honest, I am distracting myself," I say.

"Interesting. Well, let me entertain you. It is rare that I entrap a woman with debate."

There's a long pause, and in that moment I almost ask the question he's dying for me to voice, but that would invite a different sort of conversation. My eyebrow shoots up in challenge. "By all means, go ahead."

He chuckles. "You are a slippery fairy, always evading my neatly placed traps." He leans against the windowsill, his stance so disarming and at the same time suave that I have to hold myself back from taking a step closer to him. "There are many different types of love. There's the love you have for God, for your family, for a wife, and for a pretty face." I ignore his pointed stare as he pauses at this point. "There's love of charity and love of greed. Since love cannot be wholly good, I have laid it apart from virtue, which is pure goodness."

"I understand. You present a very good case. Now what I must puzzle out is why would you hide behind such a motto?"

"Hide?" He is perplexed, crossing his arms in front of his chest. My attention is drawn to the heavy gold chain around his neck with stones of jet larger than my thumb.

"You are eager to hide behind a veneer of innocence and goodness, but look at you, my lord. The handful of times I have spoken to you, your intentions were hardly pure."

He closes his eyes as if he's hurt. When he looks up again, I am taken aback by the green intensity in his stare. "We've done more than just talk." He holds up his arm in front of him. "I distinctly remember this appendage wrapped around your waist as I rescued you soaking wet from the clutches of that river."

My spine stiffens. "Now I find myself wishing you had let it carry me away. But you have proven my point. So why the motto?"

"Should a man not have a goal to strive for?" He gives me his characteristic half-smile. "Don't be cross with me, Lady Bess. I hardly know a man who would not be eager to flirt with you. Yet this brings us back around to my initial question. Why is it only me that makes you flinch?" As if to prove his point, he reaches out his hand toward me as though he were about to cup my face. Before I can stop myself, I have stepped back. Grateful for the dim light, at least I know he cannot notice how flushed I am.

He doesn't come closer, but his smile widens. "See. Tell me how I can win your good favour."

"If I say you have it, then will you leave me alone?" The question comes out a bit too breathless for my liking. I glance around us. Beyond the odd servant walking by, we are still very much alone.

"No. I don't think I could. But please add honesty back on to my list of traits."

"I'm not some conquest for you to make."

He shakes his head as if my words amuse him. "If I were trying to make a conquest of you, then you would know it, my lady."

"Your swaggering is unattractive."

"I'll make a note to keep it in check."

"That wasn't—" Then I frown. Why am I still here

arguing with him? What do I have to gain? The longer I linger the more he will suspect the truth. I turn tail to walk back to the great hall. Before I have gone more than a step, his hand is on mine. He doesn't close the distance between us, yet I can hear his breathing growing heavier as he regards me.

"Perhaps that is the very point." His voice is a half whisper. "Perhaps you do wish for my attentions..."

"N-no." I am quite at a loss.

"You should know I am a man of science. I should like to conduct an experiment."

"What?" My eyes widen as his words sink in.

"Nothing dreadful." His eyes are twinkling. "In fact, I suspect you might enjoy it."

"I don't think..."

"I just need to step closer and..."

I grow light-headed at the thought that he's going to kiss me. My imagination takes it further than that. I cannot even scold myself for such sinful thoughts.

He says nothing. His hand leaves mine and travels up to my face. His fingers stroke my cheek. "Just as I thought. You are blushing."

"A fever." I am quick to excuse myself. "You will have to excuse me."

"You have nothing to fear from me, Elizabeth. I am a tease and a flirt, but I have nothing but the best of intentions toward you."

Licking my lips, I gather my senses. It's easy for me to turn the heat in my veins into anger. "Then you have a funny way of showing it. My virtuous lord. I am growing to despise you."

He nods his head. "Next time our debate must be on the topic of hate..." He steps closer. I feel the tickle of his beard against my ear as he leans in to whisper, "And how close it is to love."

The resounding sound of my slap fills the empty corridor. He touches his cheek lightly, but his expression is filled with mirth rather than anger.

"I deserve that."

"And more."

He nods. His expression turns dark, and my knees feel weak. I fear I shall collapse under the weight of his stare.

The next moment bravery overcomes me and my lips are pressed against his. He doesn't pull away but neither does he make a move to draw me closer. I deepen the kiss until he moans against me. As I pull away, I can see from his unveiled expression that I have won this game.

"There, my lord," I say in my haughtiest tone. "I believe I have proven that you are also eager for my attentions."

"Was that ever in doubt, Bess?" Now he pulls me to him, tilting my head back. "I told you there's not a man in England who would refuse you."

I open my mouth to argue, but he silences me with another kiss. There's something delicious about the way he presses into me as he manoeuvres us into the darkness of the alcove hidden from sight. He's good at this. Too good. How many women has he done this with?

But as he nips my lower lip, I find I don't care. I need this moment to last an eternity. My back is pressed against the cold stone, yet it does nothing to douse the heat coiling within me. I shudder when his free hand trails down my neck over my collarbone. His lips follow, leaving goose bumps in their wake. He returns to my lips but hesitates.

In response I pull him closer. I pay him back in kind and run my nails through his hair. We are locked in a fierce battle, our victories determined by the sounds we elicit from each other. The soft groans and sighs.

A dose of reality hits me as he takes a moment to catch his breath.

"Say nothing about this to anyone," I beseech him. "It was a—"

"Don't you dare say it was a mistake," he whispers, muttering against the nape of my neck. I suppress a fresh shudder, knowing it would only encourage him more.

"I must go." I pull away. "This isn't meant to be an invitation. It was an experiment. One that is not to be repeated."

"If that is your wish," he drawls, but I see he is collecting himself. In the next breath, he disappears behind the polite mask of the courtier. "Your headdress is askew."

I rush to fix it but only manage to make it slip further.

"Allow me, my lady," he offers as though he were a gallant and not a knave. His fingers on my head are enough to make me hesitate. He cups my face, urging me to look up at him. I comply. For the last time, I add to myself.

"You did nothing wrong."

I cannot help but laugh. "Perhaps shamelessness is a curse in my family. I have always wondered why my mother would agree to be the mistress of a king."

"You have not—"

I cut him off with a glare. "Spare me the reassurances. I know I am not a ruined woman, and even if I was"—I shrug— "I acted of my own volition and curiosity. Not yours."

He studies my face and then pulls away once he is satisfied.

I move away from him. My steps are leaden. Then I halt and look over my shoulder. "Promise me you won't boast to anyone of what happened this evening."

He places a hand over his heart and bows. "It goes without saying." He clears his throat. "I am not without heart. The fact you had to even ask wounds me. You don't know me at all."

I turn away from him. "Exactly. I don't know you at all, and I would prefer to not be made a laughingstock." Then, catching the pain of rejection in his eyes, I add, "You are not a black-hearted villain. I do not hate you."

Fearing prolonging this conversation any longer would end with us back in the darkness of that alcove, I force myself forward.

CHAPTER 5

AUTUMN 1587-1588

S haking, my hand grips the desk for support as I reread the letter. It's short and painfully devoid of information, but the message is plain as day: my mother is dead.

Lady Holland comes up behind me. When her hand touches my shoulders, I convulse into sobs that rack my whole body.

"Dearest Lady Bess, what is the matter?"

I can hear the rising panic in her voice, but nothing can reach me now. I let the tears come, and only when my eyes are dry do I look up. My mind is a haze of sadness and guilt. Had my mother been ill but hidden it from me? The letter must have fallen out of my hand at some point because Lady Holland has handed it to Catherine Howard.

Her hands are still rubbing my back in slow circles. I am both grateful for the contact and resentful of it. I need answers. The note from my sister is so devoid of any emotions I can't wrap my mind around the news.

The two women lead me to my bedroom. They strip away my petticoat and gown and pull at the laces of my girdle. I am in my night shift and tucked into bed.

"Rest, we shall call the physician to come to you."

I turn away from them, unable to do more than resume my crying.

This pattern continues for the rest of the night. Every time I feel my tears are spent, I find fresh ones springing from my eyes.

When sunlight floods the maids' chamber, I awake with everyone else. The mundane tasks of getting ready keep me occupied. I feel the guilt rising at the back of my throat, but I try to assure myself that I have no choice but to go on living. I remind myself that I am a grown woman who was lucky to have had her mother for so long. Yet it doesn't make me feel any better. Fearing any sad look or hearing condolences, I avoid making eye contact with anyone and move through my duties with a stiffness that is unlike me.

As we process to Mass, the queen summons me to her side.

I curtsy and wait for her to speak.

"News of the sudden loss of your mother fills me with sadness. I hope you shall find the strength to bear your grief with dignity."

I nod my head. What else can I do? How can I open my heart to this impeccable woman?

"You may go home for the funeral if you wish," she says, her voice calm and collected.

"I-I don't even know when it will be held, Your Majesty. Nor how she died. I hadn't even known she was ill."

I watch, dumbfounded, as the queen takes my hand in hers and gives it a light pat. I can feel the weight of her ringed fingers anchoring me to the here and now.

"You shall write to your family and you shall discover everything that you need to know. I excuse you from your duties today. Take time to mourn and don't fret, child. It's God's will."

I nod again, wishing I could explain how grateful I am to her for this.

As the priest recites his liturgy, I find myself paying attention to his every word, picking them apart for some hidden meaning. There is solace in the choir and the familiar words.

After Mass I return to my rooms and begin penning a letter to my brother Arthur. I never get the chance to send it before a letter arrives for me. I kiss Arthur's seal before breaking it and read.

Dearest sister,

By now news has reached you that our beloved mother has passed away. We must remember to rejoice that she is with our lord and saviour now. Earthly woes and troubles cannot touch her.

We saw her often. There were no signs that there was anything amiss. I have spoken to Adrian Stokes at length and questioned her maids and household. None can point to any one thing. She went to bed early on Saturday night and in the morning her maid found her. She died quietly and wasn't in pain. We must be comforted that she didn't suffer long—though I did not believe the news when I was first told. I can only imagine how you feel. We will bury her at the family priory beside father. Stokes cannot protest this. I don't know if you can travel, but the roads are bad this time of year. Mud is three inches deep and the wind is cold and biting. I'd prefer to know you are safe, but if you feel that you need to be here then I will not stop you. We will bury her on the 17th of November. I pray you are well. We are in shock and mourning, but we are well. I have enclosed our mother's rosary with this letter. She would have wanted you to have it.

Your dearest brother,

Arthur

I bite my lower lip and look around. There is no enclosed package. Has someone taken it?

I leave the room, tying the robe tightly around me, and summon the usher who delivered the letter to me.

"There was no package with the sealed letter, I swear," he says.

My eyes continue to narrow, and he takes a step back. It takes me a moment to realise this man is actually intimidated by me. I didn't know I had it in me. Undaunted, I press forward.

"There must have been because my brother says he included one with this letter. Go and find it. If I discover you stole it, I will make sure the queen has you locked in the fleet prison." He opens his mouth to protest, but I cut him off. "Yes, the fleet prison. I don't care whose brother or uncle or cousin you are. The tower would be too good for you if you stole from a dead woman."

That felt ridiculously good. The man, on the other hand, is quaking and pale.

"Lady, I swear..."

"What's going on here?"

I go still at the sound of his familiar voice. It's been months since I have been in the same room as Raleigh and weeks since I spied him return to court. The queen graciously gifted him property in Ireland and he took a trip to visit that lush land. Once he returned, the queen had other duties for him to take up.

"Why are you here?" I can't hold back my scathing tone.

He looks amused, which only angers me further. "Leave, young master. I'll take care of this hellcat."

"This is no laughing matter," I say, all but shouting.

"Lady Bess, let him leave. You've scared the wits out of him, so I doubt he will be of any help to you anyway. I shall assist you."

I cross my arms over my chest, but I give a curt nod.

Once he is gone he turns to me, his eyebrow high in question. "Care to tell me what this was all about?"

Deflated, I collapse into the nearest seat. The corners of my eyes begin to prick and I force back the tears. I will not do this in front of him. I will not.

"This doesn't concern you," I say. My words are barely audible as the fight goes out of me.

"Actually, it does. As the queen's Captain of the

Guard, the safety and security of everyone at court is my business. Tell me, and if I can help, I will."

I open and close my mouth, but I realise he might just be more stubborn than me. He sits down across from me and manages to look calm and collected.

My eyes go from his face to his fingers clasped in front of him, and I recall how months ago he dug them into my hair. That moment is a distant memory now. I wonder if he even remembers.

"My brother sent my mother's rosary to me along with a letter. I only received the letter. I know things like this go missing in transit, but this is too precious a memento for me to lose."

He gives a sharp intake of breath that sounds more like a hiss. I watch as he gets to his feet and bows. "I will do my best to retrieve it for you. Leave it to me and try not to harass the page boys."

"He was an usher," I mutter under my breath.

He smiles at me, but there's a sadness to it as he regards me. I feel insulted by his pity. There's something too personal about him coming across me at this moment, and knowing him, I worry what he will say next.

"I am sorry for the loss of your mother. I shall do my best to retrieve your lost package. Not only because it is my duty, but because I cannot stand to see you hurt. I would lay the world bare at your feet if it would make you smile again."

I wish I could find the strength to glare at him, but instead nothing but honesty spills forth from me. "As kind as your words are, sometimes this pain is important."

His smile is sad and wistful. "I understand you more than you know. In my life, I have borne the loss of innumerable friends, colleagues, and even family members. Yet I would hurry you off this path of misery just the same. You deserve more..."

"I deserve what God gives me," I say devoutly. "Sir Raleigh, thank you for your kindness."

He leaves me alone. I almost wish he would stay. The rosary, whether retrieved or not, will not bring back my mother. It won't give me the time to say goodbye to her. Nor take away this pain that has rooted itself in my chest. I decide I will not make the trip to Coughton Court. But I swear that I shall save every penny this quarter and pay for Masses for my mother's soul. She was Catholic to her core, and I think this above all else is important to her.

A few days later, I am handed a purse with my mother's rosary inside. It's a beautiful piece, but only the tiny ruby on the end would be considered precious. The beads are well thumbed, and as I say a prayer, running my own fingers over them, I feel a strange sense of warmth from them.

Perhaps the beads had been confiscated or taken. I cannot be sure. All I know is that I'm grateful to have them in my keeping and grateful that Raleigh doesn't gloat over his discovery of them.

Time heals all things, and as I tie the rosary to my belt and wear the black band of mourning over my sleeve, I feel like I have begun the journey toward recovery.

∽

We are nearing the end of February, just as the court is preparing for the new year's celebrations in March, when my brother arrives at court. He is alight with a secret hope he does not voice. But we take time to walk in the gardens outside Nonsuch Palace and he tells me of our mother's funeral and reveals to me the nature of the first letter I received.

"Our sister Mary is not one to mince words. When I asked her what she wrote to you, I was worried how you would take the news."

I pat his arm. "Not to worry. I'm not as delicate as all of that. Only an intense guilt that I wasn't there still keeps me up at night. These things happen, but I can't help but wonder if I had stayed at Coughton—maybe—maybe things could have been different."

"It was her time. She planned to marry you off to some earl's son anyway. If you had stayed at home, then she would have sent you off somewhere anyway."

We both laugh. "Now that I'm older I understand the prudence of her desire to see me married off so well."

"Do you desire a husband? I could—"

Before Arthur can go further I stop him. "Don't worry, dear brother. I have yet to tire of the court and all its adventures."

"As I have heard," he says, giving me a sidelong glance.

I go tense, wondering what he is referring to, but I don't rise to the bait. "And you? Don't think I haven't noticed the spring in your step and the way you wait so anxiously for news every day."

Arthur runs a hand through his hair. "You've become far too observant."

I grin like a contented cat. "So there is something. Tell me, or if it's bad news, don't." My face falls even as he rushes to reassure me.

"It's Ann. She believes she might be with child, but she is not certain. There have been other times when she thought she was, but it was not meant to be."

"Oh, Arthur, how lovely for you both! I hope you shall have a bonnie babe in the nursery at Coughton and as many siblings to torment the poor thing as you desire. Or rather Lady Ann."

He bows his head. "Thank you. I shall pass on your well wishes to her. But don't think to veer me off track. There have been whispers..."

"About what?"

"You."

I am genuinely surprised. What could anyone say about me? My mind immediately drifts to Raleigh and I hope it doesn't show. "That's not much to go off of, Arthur. Stop being so coy and tell me exactly what is on your mind. Otherwise, stop tormenting me and drop it."

"Walter Raleigh."

I pride myself in the control I show holding back a gasp at having my worst fears confirmed. I remain perfectly still, though I allow my eyes to widen in surprise.

"You've been spotted getting rather close on more than one occasion. He pays special attention to you. If he were an honourable man I would not object, but you of all people must know his reputation."

"Trust me, Arthur, I know perfectly well not to meddle with him."

"He had a mistress while in Ireland. He left her pregnant. Did you know that?"

There's a painful pang in my chest at the news. I can't quite describe it. Disappointment? Anger? Betrayal? But I didn't lie when I said there was nothing between us. A few hurried kisses and sweet words mean nothing.

"Arthur, if he has shown me any special attention or favour, it was not at my behest. I will admit he was the one that helped me recover Mother's rosary. Truth be told, I never asked him where he got it from. I don't believe I even thanked him yet." I frown, making a mental note to rectify that. "So you see, if anything, I am impolite to him."

From the corner of my eye I see my brother visibly relax. I try not to feel guilty. There is no deception. An omission of facts does not make a lie. Right? I swear to myself that I shall have nothing to do with Raleigh anymore. I feel the ghost of his lips on mine and wonder how dangerously close I came to becoming like his Irish mistress.

"You can come to me with anything. I am here for you."

"Thank you," I say and mean it from the depths of my heart. "I know that. If anything should be worth reporting involving me, I shall tell you. After all, it's better you hear it from me than from those who would embellish the tale."

"I wouldn't believe them out of hand. Remember, I asked you about this business with the Captain of the Guard, didn't I?"

I chuckle, nudging him with my elbow as we round the bend. Now curiosity is getting the better of me. "What are these rumours? To be honest, I'm rather excited to hear them."

He pretends to look aghast, which only makes me laugh more. This has been the first time in a long time that I have felt so light spirited.

"Well, they say Raleigh writes verse to you and pines for your affection. They say he climbs in through the window to visit you at night and that you often sneak away from your duties to meet together in the evenings."

"My." I fan myself. "I have been busy. Whoever has been spreading these rumours has clearly never seen the thin window slits in the ladies-in-waiting's bedchamber. I doubt a sparrow could fit through them."

We stop to allow others to walk past. One of them, who I recognise as the queen's milliner, bows to me.

"I am glad to hear that." My brother blushes. "Not that I distrust you, but rather that your rooms are so well defended from cads."

I hum in agreement, but my attention is on the milliner, who is rushing down the path toward the back entrance of the palace.

"Why has parliament been summoned?" I turn back to him. "The queen has been busy ordering new clothes and accessories from every corner of England. Are we to be hosting a new foreign dignitary? She usually doesn't go through all this pomp unless that is the case."

His face goes pale and he swallows hard. Twisted up like this, Arthur's features look horrendous.

"What?"

"The Spanish," he whispers. "The queen has ordered parliament to pass a special bill to call for a levy to pay for fortifications and arms."

"They are coming? After all this time?" My heart skips a beat. The death of my mother has distracted me more than I thought. Perhaps if I had greased the right palms and asked the right questions, I would've known this by now.

The Spanish threat has been hanging over our heads for years. We had all hoped that the death of Mary Stuart would lessen their willingness to come to our shores. Instead, it has invigorated them. I suppose regardless of what we did, King Philip would attempt to capture England. Years ago he tried to do it through marriage. Among his many kingdoms England would certainly not be the best or richest, but his personal vendetta against our queen makes him relentless in his pursuit.

Perhaps even after all this time he feels the sting of his rejection. Hypocrite.

"What shall happen if they do come? How can we fight them off?"

He looks unsure and his hesitation to answer tells me everything. England is a small island nation. Our Protestant allies are already besieged by war on all corners, and our Catholic supporters will not lift a finger against Spain, which now has the approval of the Holy Father in Rome.

"We are outnumbered. Only God and the common people can help turn the tide in our favour."

Out of frustration I kick at a stone in our path and watch it go sailing. It's satisfying, though childish of me. "Our queen has never failed to rally people to her cause. I have faith in her."

"As do I," he assures me, but I can hear the doubt in his voice. Even if every man, woman, and child were to take up arms against the Spanish, would it be enough? We are far less well provisioned than they are. These would also be seasoned soldiers led by an impeccable commander who defeated us in the Netherlands count-less times.

"I should return to the queen's side. Thank you for your news, and don't let this news taint your happiness. A child is a wonderful thing to hope for."

He kisses my forehead. "Thank you. Take care of yourself, Bess. Don't lose heart."

I smile and retreat back the way we came. It's easier said than done of course. But I shall do my best.

In a few weeks the Spanish invasion is all anyone can speak about. From the servers who pour the wine and the spit boys in the kitchen to the dukes and lords of the land, everyone's mind is turned to war.

The queen presents a mask of cool collected fury to the world. She does not show an ounce of fear or hesitation as she dresses each day or rides out on hunts. In the afternoons, she is sequestered with her councillors, and builders come to her with plans from every corner of the country.

Sir Francis Walsingham has sent out his men into every port and seaside village all around England. Soon beacons are set up and will alert us the minute the Spanish are sighted. Others tend to the English fleet. Our navy is well stocked and bolstered by ships built for Raleigh and Drake.

The queen's loyal pug is remorseful at being pulled away from her side.

Leicester is the queen's shadow once more, but soon we know he will have to leave to lead the English army. None of us dare comment on his failing health, but he puts forth a brave facade as he parades out with his men. He leaves his nephew Essex behind to protect the queen and keep her company.

Cecil sends envoys to Scotland to get them to agree to not allow the Spanish to use Scotland as a base to start their invasion. Usually, we would have much to fear from Scotland, but King James, the queen's nearest relation, is wise to the fact that if Spain manages to capture England, then his chances of gaining the English throne die as well. He will remain loyal as long as the queen continues to tempt him with naming him her heir.

We, the ladies of her household, cannot do much but wait. Of course our needles and scissors fly as we stitch away at banners for our soldiers and flags. Some of us make bandages and other provisions, but in the scheme of things this is nothing.

In the evenings, there's a sense of wild abandon. Nothing matters as we sit around the presence hall with no pageants or plays or masques to put on. Someone plays the lute; others gamble at cards. All the while conversation and wine flow in a never-ending stream.

Left to our own devices like this, we begin to run wild as fear tightens its grip on us. More often than not I spy a lady sneaking out of the privy chamber. She often returns with ruffled clothes and her hair down. There's no denying she's met with a lover, and I can only envy her the distraction from all this dismay. Normally, the queen would be quick to reprimand and check our behaviour, but she faces sleepless nights trying to fight for her throne. We help her dress and bathe and look as regal as we can manage, but then we are dismissed. The longer we go on like this without supervision, the braver we become. Many are summoned home back to the country. Fear of the Spanish army and the havoc they will wreak upon us is taking hold of many people.

The gentlemen of the court come to dine in private with us. The queen's apartments begin to look closer to a bordello than a place of refinement.

One of these nights, I am perched up on the windowsill overlooking the palace and peeking up at the night sky when I hear cheers behind me as someone joins our little party.

I twist myself around and my heart nearly stops

when I spy a strangely sombre Raleigh dressed head to toe in a dark blue suit. I don't suppose he has noticed me and I am quick to turn away, trying to ignore how my heart flutters at the thought that he is here.

As I struggle to contain my emotions, I focus instead on Lady Arabella's beautiful playing. She has a special way with music. As minutes tick by and turn into hours and I am still left alone to my own devices, I stop tensing my shoulders. He has forgotten about me. This is a good thing, I remind myself. My brother's warning rings in my mind.

At last, feeling peckish, I slide from my seat, ignoring someone's call to join a card game, and go to the cupboard where a dish of sweetmeats awaits. I pick apart the crust, enjoying the buttery taste, when I see a flash of blue approaching from the corner of my eye.

Ignoring it, I try to move to the other side of the room as stealthily as I can. Of course this is a hopeless course of action. Walter Raleigh is a trained strategist—it doesn't take long for him to cross my path.

He bows his head to me in greeting.

"Lady Bess, it's been far too long."

His tone is too familiar and engaging.

"I never got the chance to thank you for finding my mother's rosary." I interrupt whatever he's about to say. My hand goes to my waist, where it rests against my hip. "I'm afraid that was impolite of me."

His eyes flash playfully at the challenge I pose. "Non-sense. It was my duty."

"If you'll excuse me." I curtsy to him and leave, aware

that he has drawn attention to us. This revelation only causes me more embarrassment.

I take a seat beside Lady Holland and watch her play at cards. When she invites me to join her game, I shake my head and yawn. Lady Anne walks past, asking if anyone wishes for a cup of wine, and I raise my hand.

When a cup is proffered to me over my shoulder, I take it with thanks. The wine inside is a deep blood-red colour. I take a delicate sip and am surprised by the fragrance and sweetness.

"Delicious," I say, licking my lower lip. When I look over my shoulder, I see a triumphant Raleigh standing there playing the part of a servant.

"Having control over the imports of wines comes with several boons," he says. "For instance, I can serve my friends with only the finest."

"We are friends?" I arch a delicately sculpted eyebrow.

"I told you we were." He takes my speaking to him as permission to sit on a stool behind me. "Why are you not joining in?"

"I prefer to watch," I say, not wishing to reveal how short of funds I truly am. "Besides, now I have this delicious wine to entertain me."

His smile is rueful. A growing unsettling feeling overcomes the apathy that filled me this evening. One day I would like to sit down with myself and examine where this feeling comes from.

Regardless of attempts to remove him from my side, he stays glued there. Only when I rise to retire for the night with a few of the other ladies-in-waiting are we separated.

As I bid him good night, I see that he is on the precipice of saying something, but he holds himself back. I wish I could peek inside his mind and see what lies there.

The bells in London peal back.

There is a great sense of panic as word spreads that the Armada is upon us. The queen is locked away in her chambers. We know that the council is divided on what she should do. Some say she should flee into hiding; others want her to stay. Neither side can decide where she should go, however.

Some ladies of her bedchamber are beside themselves about what will happen to them. Most are regretting not going home while they could have. But I am certain that the queen will not flee like a coward. She is not the sort of woman who cowers. Besides, the alternative would be even more unpalatable—look at what happened to her cousin when she sought refuge. In her shoes I would choose to stay and fight. Rather to go down fighting like a warrior of old than to die in disgrace somewhere far from home.

I flee the queen's apartments and wander around one of several inner courtyards that the queen has remodelled. As I marvel at the budding greenery, I am reminded that the plants don't know war is coming.

Blood might be shed in this very courtyard, yet nature will keep on growing.

A shiver passes through me at the thought of these white stones stained red.

These are not the thoughts of a young woman approaching her twenty-fourth year. I should be giggling over suitors, practicing the latest dance steps, and discussing the latest fashions.

Unfortunately, my taste for such things has turned to ash in my mouth. Under these circumstances, this would be a natural reaction. However, the truth is far more sinister. The secret I've been harbouring in my heart is festering like an open wound. I find it difficult to sleep, and my appetite is gone.

For in these dark days all I can think about is Raleigh.

CHAPTER 6

SPRING 1588 - AUTUMN 1588

With destruction knocking at our door, the temptation to give in to all my desires is becoming harder to ignore. I partake in gambling and lose a scary amount of money on cards. In the evenings, I lie in bed thinking of his kisses and his touch. I fear for him. He might die tomorrow before I've had the chance—no. I cannot even bring myself to voice the terrible desire that's been haunting me ever since that evening long ago.

To keep myself busy I wander around the closed off courtyards or walk through the palace, aimlessly searching out distraction.

What is it about Sir Walter Raleigh that has set my heart aflame and driven me to such distraction? He certainly has done nothing to deserve it. I cannot even finish this thought without remembering the way his breath fanned across my skin.

Today, I stroll towards his apartments.

I have gone insane.

Yet with every step I am getting closer. He might have left for his post already. Even if he is there, what will I do? Would I be so brazen as to ask to speak to him?

Before I can answer myself I am standing in front of his door. My hand, clenched into a fist, reaches out.

There's a lump in my throat that I cannot force down.

Insanity—this is what it must feel like.

I am saved from deciding by the opening of the door. A servant comes traipsing out and is forced to come to a sudden halt lest he crash into me.

"Pardon me, my lady." He bows. "May I assist you in some way?"

All my training as a courtier comes in handy as I become strangely calm. "Is your master, Sir Walter, here? I have a message from the queen." The lie comes quickly as if I had rehearsed it.

"He is." He cranes his head to look behind him. "At this very moment he's preparing to leave. I can pass your message along if you wish."

"I-I...that's—"

I am saved from my stuttering by the appearance of Raleigh himself in the doorway. If he is surprised to see me, he doesn't let it show on his face.

"Saddler, what is this? I sent you on an urgent errand."

"But, sir, the lady..."

"Off you go. I'll hear the queen's message myself. You have other duties to attend to." Raleigh's voice is a rolling drawl.

I watch the servant scamper off. Raleigh pushes open the door wider.

"Are you coming in, or are you planning on standing there gaping like a fish all day?"

Without thinking, I step through the doorway, and so with one act I destroy my reputation.

Raleigh doesn't linger but moves about his business. He's sorting through papers on his desk and looking over his trunks.

Nerves are getting the better of me, and I bite my lower lip to stop myself from shaking.

"Why are you here, Bess?" he says. I envy him for his calmness. Then again, if rumours are to be believed, being alone in a room with a woman is not uncommon for him.

I look up to see him watching me from the corner of his eyes.

"The queen—"

He closes the lid on one of the trunks, placing his foot on the lid to hold it in place as he locks it in place. I admire the outline of his calf and the strength of his arms as he pulls the straps tight.

"We both know that is a lie."

I open my mouth to protest.

But he fixes me with one of his stares. "Enough with the games. I was just at the queen's side before you appeared. Seeing as she locked herself in the privy council room with Walsingham and Cecil, I doubt you could have seen her or received instructions from her."

Every word is a nail in my coffin. I cannot bear the

way he studies me from across the room as if he can guess my thoughts.

This was a mistake. I take a step back.

"Bess. Answer me." His tone is at once deliciously commanding and yet warm.

"The war. All I could think of is that you might perish."

"Do you think so little of my abilities?"

"The Spanish hate you. If they get their hands on you..."

He nods and continues to move about the room.

I am dumbfounded. It doesn't help that I'm trying to process my own emotions, complicated and hazy as they are. Closing my eyes, I try to steady my breathing and gather my wits.

The touch at my shoulder makes me whip around. I don't expect him to be so close. The back of his hand rises to my temple.

"If I recall, you are prone to fevers. Are you feeling well?"

My voice has abandoned me, so I am forced to bob my head. I try to bat his hand away from me, but he only captures it in his other hand.

"Tell me again why you are here." He leans forward inch by inch, his eyes never leaving mine. I've never heard of a seduction like this before.

"The war."

He hums against the nape of my neck. He hovers there. I hear every inhalation and feel every exhalation. My legs go weak as goose bumps spread over my skin. An image of exactly what I want enters my mind. My thoughts are cut off as he pulls away, leaving me feeling exposed in the worst way.

Though his eyes are now a dark stormy green, he is very much composed. He steps away again. Returning to his business.

"Bess. I am a soldier, a sailor. Many things. I can tell you now that you are acting rashly and out of fear."

I am pleased to note the roughness in his voice. Being so close to me has not left him quite as unaffected as he looks. But I can't understand—

"You should leave."

Whatever I had been expecting, it was not this. The possibility that I misjudged his interest in me makes my cheeks burn red with embarrassment.

My face twists in what I imagine is an unflattering way as I try and fail to disguise my emotions. The urge to flee is growing, but my stubbornness rises to meet it. I won't be dismissed like this.

Raleigh stops what he is doing and lets out a sigh. "You will regret coming here, and I could never forgive myself for taking advantage."

Hope rekindled, I am about to rush to reassure him that I am a woman who knows her own mind. But the more I think about it, the urge to laugh at the ridiculousness of this situation is overwhelming. Isn't he supposed to be a great womaniser? How is it that I am the one prostrating myself at his feet? That's when another more dangerous thought creeps forward.

"Why?" The question whips out at him. He's taken

off guard and I press my advantage home. "Why would you care if I come to regret meeting you in your rooms like this?"

He says nothing, but he has turned away from me and I can no longer make out the subtle nuances of his expression.

Brazenly, I step closer to him. Now it is I who touches his shoulder. "Are you not a cold-hearted seducer? Have you not done this hundreds of times? Why should you care about one more, on the eve of battle no less?"

He chuckles. It's a crude sound from the back of his throat. "So I am just a means to an end?"

"Answer the question," I say firmly.

He smirks. "What would you like me to say?"

"The truth." I place my hand over his heart, feeling the thread of the embroidered buck on his jacket. My heart leaps into my throat, and no matter how I try to steady myself my breathing becomes erratic.

He covers my hand with his but does not remove it or push me away. Our eyes are locked on each other.

"I could joke that I am not some stud at market." He winces at the crudeness of his own words. "But the truth. The truth is that I fear once our—business—is concluded you will hate me, and I cannot bear to think of you hating me. The consequences..." He trails off at my smile.

"You do care." I step even closer to him, tilting my head up. "The moment I stepped into this room I was beyond caring about consequences. I want you. I want this. If the whole world burns up tomorrow, I want to die with the taste of your lips on mine. If we are saved, then I want to never forget the touch of your hand." My arm snakes up around his neck, and gently I pull him closer to me.

He obliges, but when his lips meet mine, rather than smoulder the fire burning within me, he ignites it. Any lingering worries and hesitations disappear with his continued teasing kisses. I want more and groan out my frustration. Misinterpreting the sound, he stills. Impatient, I nip his bottom lip, intent on showing him my disappointment at the interruption. His lips curl into a smile, no doubt pleased to have me yearning for his touch, but I quickly forgive him as he starts trailing kisses down my cheekbone.

It's hard to keep track of his movements. One moment his hand is on my waist, the next it's pulling the pins holding my hairnet in place.

They fall to the floor with a resounding ping. He pulls one after another out. They go the same way as the first. The process is slow but the result rewarding. My hair, now free from the confines of my headdress, tumbles down my back. My hair is not very dark nor very fair, as is the fashion, yet I have no doubt that he desires me as he steps back to admire me. The next moment he beckons me forward.

Decency and honour have long since been abandoned. I am not afraid. My only goal is to quench this growing thirst in my body.

Unabashed, I obey, letting my hips sway provocatively, and I am rewarded by a renewal of his attentions.

"You are certain?" His whisper is constrained as he pauses once more. His hands comb through my hair in slow, deliberate movements.

"Whether or not we continue this, I am ruined. I might as well get some pleasure out of this."

He taps my nose. "What of me and my reputation? I wonder if at this moment any man will do for you?"

My mind is whirling in a fog of desire as he continues this game of coming forward and pulling back. My patience is running thin.

I do my best to be coy. "Do you need assurances, my love?"

"I wouldn't mind." He continues to tease. "Some compliments would be nice..."

Tiring of this game, I growl in annoyance, and he silences me with a crushing kiss.

Time has no meaning as we continue to play. I am an eager student and a quick study. It's not long before I have him melting at my touch.

When at last we disentangle our limbs from each other, I am at a loss for what to say. Is the pleasure of this act always so—pronounced? My philosophical musings are put on hold as Raleigh leaves the bed. He is slipping on his hose and looks as if he's about to bolt before remembering these are his rooms.

I prop myself on my elbows and give him a lazy half-smile. "You were wrong."

"About?" His voice is strained.

"I don't regret this and I never shall."

He sits down on the side of the bed near me, cupping my face.

"In this matter, I happily concede defeat," he says, now kissing both cheeks. "I wish we had more time, but I must go, and you must return before anyone notices you have gone."

Something tells me that I could protest and keep him at my side, but I don't. After all, I am still a practical woman. It would suit me to have this be a secret between the two of us.

Nor am I ready to discuss what happened or where our actions might take us. There's no sense in hearing empty promises of love and affection either. He didn't seduce me with promises of marriage, nor did he trick me into coming to him on some false pretence. If anything, I was the culprit, and so it's only fair I bear the consequences.

With soft practiced hands he sets about helping me dress. When at last we come to my hair I sit on the edge of the bed and begin plaiting my hair. He stops me with a touch of his hands and shifts so he's now sitting directly behind me. The heat of his body so close to my own is awakening my desire. With a frown I concede to his skilled hands as I wrestle down my emotions. Of course this is a mistake. His touch—without meaning to—sends fresh shivers coursing through me. When he is done, his fingertips linger on the naked skin of my neck. My grip tightens on the headdress on my lap, knowing I should pass it to him but finding myself unable to. There would be something so final about it.

"You have such fine soft hair," he whispers, kissing my shoulder.

"Of all the things I've been complimented on, it's never been that." I look over my shoulder. His eyes are dark with unconcealed want.

"Tell me what your other beaus compliment you on then." He reaches around me and pulls the headdress from my tight hold. My gaze follows his every move as he inspects it.

"Let me see. There are my delicate hands."

He scoffs. I struggle to hide a smile and continue.

"My full lips. Almond-shaped eyes. Shapely figure..."

"That last one is a lie. It goes far beyond the language one should use with a lady. Besides, it's such an uninspired and obvious thing to remark upon."

I chuckle, hearing the twinge of jealousy in his tone. Motioning for him to carry on with his task, I look forward again. "You caught me. There was no other that would dare—besides you."

At the intake of breath behind me, I know he has recalled the words of admiration he lavished on me just moments ago.

He tsks. "Well, I must do better next time."

My heart skips a beat. I almost say something, but I hold back.

At last my headdress is pinned into place. I stand, smoothing out the pleats of my skirt, and spin for his inspection.

He hums appreciatively, as if we have all the time in

the world. "None would be the wiser. If it wasn't for the rosiness in your cheeks."

I shrug. "I suppose that can't be helped."

Raleigh shows me out through a secret passageway. Before I disappear out the door, he says, "You will be safe. Rest assured England will not fall to the likes of the Spanish."

"Can you promise that you will also return safely to court?"

His silence speaks volumes.

On impulse I kiss him again. "Come back," I say, leaving no room for discussion.

As I leave I cannot help but glance back. He's watching me as intently as I am him. For a moment I falter. Seeing this, he mouths, "Go," and there's nothing for me to do but obey.

By a stroke of luck no one has noted my absence, or at least they don't comment on it. From the conversation and quiet praying around the room I know that everyone is distracted by the prospect of war. It's terrifying to imagine London brought to its knees as Spanish soldiers come marching through the streets looting and burning as they did when they laid siege to Rome. If they did not respect that holy city, what will they do to London? Especially since they consider England and all its people heretics.

My mind drifts, but my body remains anchored by

what transpired between Raleigh and me. As I wash for the evening I spy a love mark on the inside of my wrist. As the memories come crashing back I am left stunned—both at my depravity and the intimacy we shared. That night sleep evades me, but I am not alone, as most of us are left tossing and turning until the early hours of the morning.

As we dress and assemble for Mass we are all frozen with anxiety, and only the news from the queen that she will ride out to meet with the English army pulls us out of our dark thoughts.

Admiral Lord Howard of Effingham has sent his private secretary to receive instructions and reassure the queen that her navy is ready to face all enemies.

When we enter the queen's chambers, carrying her clothes for the day and everything for her toilette, we find her hunched over her writing desk.

At first I think she is crying, and in silence we troop in. Only then can I hear the scratch of her pen. She straightens up and looks over her work. Salting the ink to dry it faster, she turns to us, her eyes sparking with zeal. She's a woman with a singular purpose and she has no doubt she will succeed.

"Someone bring the bishop to see me immediately."

"Your Majesty?" Catherine Howard gingerly takes a step forward. Now I understand she thinks the queen has lost her mind.

"Summon him," the queen clips. "I wish him to read this special prayer of intercession."

"At once." Another lady steps forward and bows.

We begin to dress her. The queen is calm, and while this should put us all at ease, it seems to have the opposite effect. We are all unnerved in the face of her confidence of victory.

As she examines herself in the mirror and asks for a different ruff for her outfit, she finally catches our wide-eyed expressions.

Queen Elizabeth looks from one to another and then laughs. "Why do you all look as if you have seen a ghost? Come, I shall have none of this among my own ladies. Are you so easily cowed?"

We look at each other and then do our best to exude even a fraction of her confidence.

Days of uneasiness follow as we await news. For now the Spanish have not landed. We begin to hope that a miracle has taken place.

I find myself in awe of the queen. Derogatory pamphlets are scattered across London, no doubt by Spanish spies. They question her parentage, her ability to lead, and call her a heretic that should be expelled from Christendom.

Walsingham hunts down the culprits, but the queen merely shrugs. Even if half the things written on that paper were true, it doesn't mean anything, for here she stands. Elizabeth Tudor has shown she belongs on the English throne.

The first inkling of good news reaches us. Drake has

managed to scatter the Spanish fleet. Many of their ships were lost to fire and hundreds more to the skill of our English sailors.

Despite the cheers that go up in the great hall, the queen does not smile.

"Parma is still waiting on the other side of the channel with his army," she says, tapping her long fingers on the armrest of her makeshift throne. She waits for silence before speaking again. "I shall ride out to be with the army when Parma lands," she says to us, waiting for one of us to dare gainsay her.

After a moment of stunned silence, a chorus of noes sounds out.

"You cannot do so, Your Majesty. Your safety is paramount above all else," Cecil says with a bow. He's the only one brave enough to speak his mind.

The queen shakes her head. There's a swell of passion in her eyes as she stands. "England's safety is above all my first priority. I've been placed on this throne by God for this very reason." She stops to regard us, her ladies-in-waiting and gentlewomen of the bedchamber. "I would be a poor mistress to you if I asked you to accompany me. So by my command I order you to retreat to St. James Palace for your protection."

"You shall join us there? After?" I bravely say, with my head downcast.

"God willing."

"Amen," we all say. The councillors share a look and I know they are already planning how to stop her.

The councillors and advisors surrounding the queen prevail over her good sense and she doesn't embark for the south coast to be with her main army. Instead, Leicester proposes she come visit the army stationed at Tilbury, a comfortable distance inland. She agrees to retreat to St. James Palace after this.

Of course, while we are running about trying to be useful and pretend we are calm, events overtake us.

The English fleet following the Spanish to Calais manages to sabotage their fleet with fire and cannon, scattering the large Spanish galleys. Parma is unable to travel.

We help the queen dress in a white shimmering gown. Two women carry a silver cuirass made especially for her. It's more an ornament than actual armour. The silver breastplate would not defend her against a blow, but to see her wearing it makes her look like a Valkyrie from the old legends.

She wears a wig with hair braided and coiled around her head like a crown of flame.

None of us can take our eyes off her as she is helped into the litter to take her to Tilbury.

Once there, she will enter the camp riding a horse of pure white. The sword of state and a helmet made for her will be carried behind her. She wants to make a statement, and Leicester is happy to arrange such a spectacle.

We hear from second-hand accounts how the soldiers got to their knees as she walked among them, calling out, "God save Your Majesty!"

The next day she returned and gave a heart-wrenching speech to the troops. Her chaplain was waiting on hand to record her words. Soon all the printers are ensuring her words are immortalised by ink and paper.

I find the coins to buy a copy of my own. I read it over and over again and marvel at the power behind such a short speech. Having been so long in her presence, I can hear her tone and imagine her features as she must have said every word.

"I have the body of a weak and feeble woman?" Lady Holland says, reading over my shoulder. She laughs. The sound is cold and clipped. "She must have forgotten how she rode us and the rest of her courtiers ragged this summer."

I nudge her. This is not the time for humour, but she doesn't seem to notice my growing irritation.

"Why are we always disregarding our strengths? It's infuriating to know how we women suffer and toil yet must claim to be weak."

When I study her expression, I see I am mistaken. She is sincere in her angry ranting. I remind myself of the loss of her sister in childbirth the month before. She had been distraught and could barely conceal her flinching every time the priest strayed close to the topic of a woman's weakness or inherent sin.

"It's what's expected of us to say," I say, trying to make her see reason. "She would be accused of being unnatural if she were to take up the mantle of soldier and general." Seeing Lady Holland's frown, I am quick to add, "I am sure she would make a great war general, but you cannot deny that she has neither the training nor skill on the battlefield. Her majesty is wise to let other more experienced persons take the lead in this matter. You would not appreciate if someone was to tell you how to embroider if they had never done it before."

Lady Holland lets out an exasperated puff of air, but the cloud of darkness lying over her face is lifting.

"She does claim she will take to the battlefield and lead the charge into battle. Do you think she will if push comes to shove?"

I think for a moment. "I don't believe these are empty words. She will never be imprisoned again. I can imagine her going down fighting."

"I wish I was brave enough," Lady Holland says in a low whisper as if she's confessing.

"Not many could."

She tilts her head, regarding me. "I don't know. You always struck me as the sort of woman who would never be gainsaid by anyone. You make up your own mind. I know that brother of yours would love to marry you off."

"He respects—"

"Respect has nothing to do with it. He fears you."

Now it's my turn to laugh. "That's preposterous. I am here to serve the queen. It's given me a certain level of freedom I might not otherwise have had."

Lady Holland looks unconvinced. "Well, either you are the luckiest woman I know or you are so strong-willed that no one can stand in your way."

"Likely the latter."

She pats my shoulder. "Just don't forget you can't face the world alone."

"I shall do my best on that account."

"Good. There's no point living like a nun for the rest of your life. Now put down that paper and come with us to play bowls on the lawn."

I frown. "Doesn't that feel inappropriate given the times?"

Lady Holland looks bemused. "What would be appropriate? Quaking in fear in corners? We've stitched enough banners and flags to last us two wars. Now let's enjoy life."

I see the wisdom of her words. It's not only the thought of war that has me in such a serious mood while at the same time I feel lost and shaken off course. But I cannot speak to anyone of Raleigh and what took place between us. Even if I could, I wouldn't know what to say. What do I want from him? And even if I knew, what if he...

Lady Holland clears her throat. I blink and look up, realising she's said something and I didn't hear.

Sheepish, I make my excuses and let her lead me outside.

Trumpets and cannon fire fill the city with noise.

The shops are closed and doors are locked.

But we are not afraid. Instead, we are celebrating a miracle that even the most confident among us had never thought possible. The Spanish are defeated. A fair number of them now lie at the bottom of the sea. In contrast, our losses have been few. A few anxious days ago, before we had any news, we were all mute with anxiety. Now we can breathe again. The citizens of England feel safe to holler and take to the streets in what is to be the start of a grand celebration.

Wild tales are spreading to every edge of the kingdom about how these invaders were repelled. The church bells ring for what feels like a whole day in thanksgiving following the news that Parma was sent scurrying back to Spain.

The likes of our Lord Admiral and Francis Drake become heroes, and their exploits are embellished overnight. The young Essex capitalises on the mood of the people and is quick to put himself front and centre. He had been put in charge of a defence force here in London, so he is perfectly positioned to kick off the celebrations as if the credit were all his for England's victory.

I can smile and applaud along with the queen and the rest of the ladies, but my joy is incomplete until I hear confirmation that Raleigh is alive.

The thrill of excitement that races through me leaves me surprised and confused. I hadn't realised the depths of my feelings until this moment. It makes me all the more nervous to see him again. Until I know where we stand, I must conquer my emotions. It's especially daunting when I, myself, don't have answers to questions I wish to ask him. Do I want to marry him? Do I want to continue this dalliance? Can I envision a future with him?

Finally I reach the crux of the issue—can I bring myself to trust him?

The answer continues to evade me, and so my restlessness grows and grows with each passing day.

Whitehall Palace at the start of September is to host the start of a series of celebrations that will end in November with Saint Elizabeth's day.

The palace is bursting at the seams with every courtier desperate to return and every other person with a good jacket eager to journey to London to celebrate one of the most monumental victories England has had since the Battle of Agincourt, when our tiny nation ruled half of France.

I am honoured more than ever to be at the queen's side and have a front-row seat to the festivities.

My brother travels from Coughton with his wife, whose growing belly is obvious to all. I congratulate the pair, and though my duties keep me at the queen's side, I make sure to see them every evening before I go to bed.

"We feared for our lives," Lady Ann says, a hand rubbing her stomach in slow repetitive circles. "I was terrified and urged Arthur to take me to Ireland or France." She laughs, but I can see on her face how even recalling the memory makes her features twist up in fear.

"Now she urged me to bring her to London. As it

turns out, my profession is to be a courier." Arthur comes to sit beside us, pretending to look exasperated. "What of you, sister? You were very brave to remain here."

"I had every faith we would be all right. More or less." I shrug. "It didn't even cross my mind to flee into France."

"That's because your French isn't nearly as good as it should be," Arthur teases.

I laugh, feeling that urge to stick out my tongue.

"Well." He claps his hands together. "What's done is done. I say a prayer for thanksgiving every day. So can you tell us what Leicester has planned? There's talk he has imported fireworks."

"How would I know what he has planned?"

"Is he not always by the queen's side? Ever since Tilbury she will not let him go far from her. If he wasn't married, I wonder if she would marry him."

Lady Ann is looking amused but interested and nods to me to join the speculation.

"I cannot venture to say what the queen would do or say. She is a private person. Regardless, at her great age there is no question of her having children. What would be the point?" I feel a blush creep up my cheeks as lewd memories of my time with Raleigh return.

Across from me Lady Ann shares a knowing glance with my brother.

"If you are ever married, perhaps you will know," Lady Ann offers and then laughs at Arthur's horrified face. "Is it shocking to think of your sister as a bride?"

He nods. "Feels more unlikely than England defeating Spain."

"But it did happen," I say with a half-smile. "Maybe you shall witness more miracles in your lifetime."

He grins and then suggests we play a game of chess.

My mind is far away, so I play poorly even with Lady Ann's assistance.

The skies are as clear as the troops assembled in front of Whitehall. Their uniforms and weapons are clean and polished so they look resplendent as the queen watches from a large window. Essex is in charge of these festivities.

Normally this would be a role reserved for her favourite. A position everyone knows Essex is desperate for, but her stepfather is the one at the queen's side. A far more intimate responsibility.

Watching him standing beside the queen, I can feel the triumph exuding from him. Yet despite this I cannot help but notice the yellow tinge to his skin and the occasional tremble of his legs as the day drags on.

How will he manage the state dinner after the jousting?

As the queen is jubilant and full of hope, no one dares point out to her that perhaps Leicester should be excused.

A blare of trumpets down below announces the competition is set to begin. Essex rides a black steed reminiscent of the one Leicester rode in his youth carrying the queen's favour. His challenger, the Earl of Cumberland, has chosen to wear black armour. This isn't a coincidence. The obvious playacting I'm about to witness frustrates me. Instead of watching, I begin to search the crowd for Raleigh.

Cumberland is swiftly defeated. We all cheer and clap as if we are surprised by the outcome. More challengers step forward, and I know that this will be a long and predictable affair. Essex will be keen to be the victor every time. The dread at this event wells up inside me and I am keen to escape.

I retreat from the gallery, making excuses to a surprised Catherine Howard that I need to use the water closet before I get free.

Walking with purpose toward the queen's apartments, no one looks twice my way. It is then I run across Walter Raleigh going in the opposite direction. He's running toward the queen but when he spots me he comes to a stop.

"Elizabeth."

He says my name as if he is reciting a prayer.

Meanwhile, I am speechless. My nights and days have been so consumed with thoughts of him that now that I am actually in his presence I don't know what to do. My head spins. Worrying I'm about to collapse, I reach out for the wall to steady myself.

In a second he is by my side. A hand on my waist, the other on my arm.

"You aren't well. I shall summon help."

"No!" The prospect of creating a fuss fills me with dread. "Please. I am well. I just need some fresh air."

"There's a balcony just over there."

"I don't think it would be wise to go somewhere alone with you right now."

He takes a step back to assess me. "If you are certain, my lady."

I wince at the formality. "Sir Francis, you took me by surprise. I hadn't thought to see you here."

"Or at all?" he presses and in response I shy away from him.

"No. That is to say, I wanted to see you. In fact, I was hoping to see you. Since I didn't see you jousting, I thought I'd be seeing you when we dine this evening."

"Ah." That simple sound makes him sound reassured.

"Why aren't you taking part?"

He smiles and begins to lead me to the terrace. It makes me forget my reservations about being alone with him. It's not that I don't trust him but rather that I don't myself.

"The queen, rightfully so, commanded no English ship leave port while the Spanish were threatening our borders, but now that order should be lifted. I need to send a ship with supplies to Virginia." Seeing my look of confusion, he adds, "The colony I started in the New World."

"So you will be leaving?"

"Not I. My captain is being sent ahead of me. Business keeps me here at court for the time being. I cannot leave for many months like I used to, or at least not for now. There's no one I trust to look after my affairs here."

He pushes open the screen lattice and invites me to step outside. I breathe in deep, revelling in the scent of the clean autumn air. My nerves steady at last and I regard him rather sheepishly.

"Thank you for taking time away from your duties to care for me."

Again that dimpled smile appears. "What kind of knight would I be if I didn't go saving damsels in distress?"

My lips quiver and my expression falls. Am I still a damsel? But I force myself to push the thought away. Out of the corner of my eye I can see he is antsy to go. My heart aches at the thought that he is done with me.

"Don't let me keep you," I say, knowing that later I might shed a few tears, but at least the wondering about our future will come to an end. Soon he shall be forgotten.

"I think you have laid a trap for me." He speaks low, his tone gruff around the edges. "Don't misunderstand me. I wish we had more time to speak, but duty compels me to leave your side. Tell me now, Elizabeth, for thoughts of you have tormented me, do you want to see me again or have you come to revile me?"

I gasp to hear my own worries spoken out loud. "I've worried about you ever since you went away. Could barely sleep. Then I realised..."

The words die in my throat as he leans forward and places a chaste kiss on my lips.

I inhale his scent, that faint smell of tobacco and sea air. The urge to wrap my arms around him to pull him closer is getting hard to ignore.

"We cannot linger," he says breathlessly. "I shall send you a message."

I nod.

"It's good to see you, Elizabeth," he adds in a hushed tone.

I stay out on the terrace listening to the distant sounds of the jousting. Soon I shall have to return, but for now the delicious memories are mine to play over and over in my head.

When I return to the queen's side, she's laughing at something Raleigh said.

"Why were you not here to greet us on our arrival in London?" the queen asks.

Raleigh bows. "You must forgive me, Your Majesty. As you can see, I have shrivelled away to nothing. Having been sent away from your side has broken me. Yet now that you have allowed me within your sight, I am once more invigorated." As if to prove his point, he performs a small leap while never fully rising from his bow.

The queen invites him to rise and lets him kiss her hand. "You are welcomed back to court, my loyal pug." She turns away from him and he takes his place among the gentlemen.

The one person the queen wants is Leicester. She is constantly leaning toward him. Even when her eyes are focused elsewhere or she is in deep conversation, her hand stretches out as if to reassure herself that he is still there.

My heart breaks for her.

As the plates of marvellous delicacies are carried off, the dancing begins. By now everyone is at least half drunk and in a cheerful mood, so when the queen motions for the musicians to start a galliard most of us take to the floor.

There are many eager supplicants for my hand. None are the man I wish for, yet with a smile I accept and let myself be twirled into one dance after another.

Toward the end of the night Adrian Gilbert, Raleigh's half-brother, approaches me with a sly smile and deep bow. "May I have the next dance?"

I nod and try not to let my disappointment show.

Only as the music ends and he bows to me does he pass a slip of paper into my hand before leaving my side.

With my heart hammering in my chest I retreat back to my seat. I take my time glancing around to see who is looking my way. A fresh dance begins. Katherine Bridges, the young fresh-faced beauty, draws all attention to her when she lets out a lyrical laugh as her partner lifts her high up into the air.

I yawn and make a great pretence of needing to step out. Only in the gallery outside do I unfurl the tiny square of paper that Gilbert put in my hand.

Tomorrow morning. Wine cellars -W.R.

I set the note afire and stamp it to ash. Uncertainty bites at my ankles as I return to the great hall. How will I be able to go undetected?

For now I put on my best performance. The noise overwhelms my senses, as do the flashing colours as the dancers whip past me.

A very tipsy Sir Henry Lee pulls me to his side. "Why are you not dancing, my lady?" he manages to ask between hiccups.

"I was," I say, smiling brightly to distract him from removing his hand from my waist. "And you, sir? Why are you not dancing?"

He leans forward, tries to wink, and trips over his own feet. I help to steady him as he laughs. "I've tasted too much of this excellent vintage. But I feel very much alone."

My eyebrow rises. I look about us. Plenty of his friends look embarrassed for him.

"Then perhaps you should return home to your London house. I am sure you'd be in good company there."

He has the decency to go pink.

"Yes! You are right," he declares in a yell. "Excellent idea."

I don't bother to curtsy before continuing on my way.

Sir Henry Lee might be the queen's champion and a preferred friend, but everyone knows about the mistress he keeps at his London house. The queen turns a blind eye to his many faults, but there is a reason she hasn't promoted him higher.

The night is long, and though I let myself get pulled into conversations and dancing, I find myself growing more and more impatient for the morning. Frustratingly, I note that a specific time wasn't specified. How early did Raleigh mean? I make a mental note to chide him.

After such a heady day of celebrating with wine flowing freely all night, the court is subdued. It is well past eight in the morning and no one is stirring. The few who are dancer's the servants who are still scampering about trying to clean up after the feasting.

As I make my way around the maze of Whitehall Palace, I pass by more than a few people who never made it to their beds and rather found comfort on the cold stone. I tiptoe around them, hoping none wake and notice me sneaking about.

Having lived for over ten years at court, I've gathered an intimate knowledge of the queen's favourite palaces. Now more than ever, I am grateful for the knowledge. I slip around a corner and go down a stairway to the wine cellar. There is one main cellar and I pray that I shall find Raleigh here.

The wine cellar at Whitehall was built in the time of the queen's father. The white stones and high ceiling create light underground. Caskets upon caskets of wine and ale are neatly arranged around the room. Large oak tables where wine might be decanted are the only other furniture in the room. No one else is here yet, so I take a moment to admire the craftsmanship of the domed ceiling. My eyes close and I say a silent prayer.

When I hear hurried steps coming down the stairs, I slip behind a pillar. I cannot breathe from fear of discovery. What excuse can I make?

Raleigh's familiar form shrouded in shadow steps into the room. Immediately I breathe a sigh of relief and I come out of my hiding place.

"You've come," he says with a smile that makes his eyes gleam. I allow him to take me into his arms and press a kiss upon my brow.

"I'm starting to regret my decision. When I heard footsteps I thought I was done for."

He clicks his tongue against the roof of his mouth. "Nonsense."

"How did you know when to come?" I frown. "You hadn't mentioned a time. To be honest, I wasn't sure I'd run into you at all."

He grins and gives me a mischievous wink as he approaches one of the wine caskets and makes a great fuss about reading the inscription. "I set a watch and my man alerted me a lady left the queen's apartments."

"You told someone who you were meeting?" My frown only deepens. Anxiety growing, but for an altogether different reason. Until now the thought that he has bragged about his conquest has not crossed my mind. He had promised, but...

"I didn't tell him who to watch out for. I took a chance. That is all," he says.

I blush. "You never told me you are a mind reader too."

He shrugs. "I know how people think. There's no magic to it."

We fall into silence as he grabs two cups from a cupboard and pours us from the casket.

"Are you sure we should?" I say, taking the cup from him.

"It's my wine." His smirk is one of unconcealed pride. "We have much to discuss. I thought it best for us to wet our beaks."

"Ha." But the retort I had is forgotten when I taste the wine. "This is delicious."

"I knew you'd like it. I've noted you prefer drier vintages."

He's teasing me. Without looking up, I add, "The older the better."

He laughs. "You wound me, madam. But I doubt you would truthfully prefer a very old decrepit variety."

"Are we still discussing wine?" I say, glancing at him from underneath my lashes.

"That would be up to you."

I set down the cup on the table with him mimicking my movements. "I assume we don't have much time."

"No," he admits, looking toward the doorway. "This was the best I could come up with in such a short amount of time. I wanted to see where things stood with us. Do you still—" He pauses, mulling over his words, then running his hand through his hair, and shakes his head. "I am hopeless. I've always considered myself a wordsmith. You may have heard compliments from the queen herself on my poetry. Yet I find myself at a loss of what to say in front of you. How do you explain that?"

"What can I say, my lord? Only you can know your own mind."

"What do you want from me?" He steps forward. "Shall I never speak to you again? Never lay eyes on you?"

I look away, unable to bear the intensity in his gaze. "I don't know what I want. But at the moment, all I can think about is your touch. So never seeing you again horrifies me."

"Tell me how I can reassure you." His tone is suggestive and I cannot help noticing that he has stepped closer still.

Gathering my courage, I face him head on, chin tilted up. "I want you to kiss me."

Raleigh's eyes widen in surprise for the briefest moment. He pretends to consider my words rather carefully, but then with a groan he swears. "I am at your command."

The next moment he has pulled me flush against him, his hand behind my head angling me up to meet his fervent kisses.

My pulse rises with each teasing lingering touch. My attraction for him turns to need. He hoists me up on one of the tables with ease. His arms on either side of me hold me steady as he lavishes me with his skilled attention.

I yearn for the press of his body against me. This fumbling is not enough, could never be enough, and yet it must never end.

He freezes above me. The sound of my beating heart is all I can hear, yet he moves off me in a flash of fabric. "Hide."

I run and hunker down behind one of the caskets just as two servants come in. They stop in their tracks seeing Raleigh here.

"My lord." They both bow in tandem but not before sharing a glance. "May we help you with something?"

I close my eyes. We've been caught. They will tell the queen or someone else who will tell the queen and I'll be ruined. I swallow hard and have to remind myself to breathe lest I faint.

Raleigh is a consummate actor. He looks at them disdainfully. "I wished to inspect the latest delivery to her majesty's cellars. Nothing can go wrong with the festivities. And you, why are you here? Not seeking to slip something into these barrels?"

One of them blanches and hurries to apologise, but the other notes that two goblets are out on the table.

Raleigh catches him looking. "I was sampling all of them. Is there a problem?" His stance changes and his tone is deeper, darker.

I cannot see his expression, but I understand I am seeing Raleigh the commander now.

The men bow. "No, of course not, sir."

"Be about your business then."

Raleigh watches them grab a barrel of ale and lug it

up the stairs without another glance his way. He pretends
to go back to tasting the wine. When at last they are gone,
he motions for me to come out.

"This is too dangerous," I whisper, all together
sobered from the brush with danger.

He smooths back my hair. "Doesn't it make it all the
more delicious?" He leans down, nipping at my lower lip,
but I push him away.

"I can't."

He lets out a heavy breath. "I know. Let me think of
something and I will find a way to send a message to you.
It will be sent through my half-brother or my nephew.
These are men I would trust with my life. I will think of
something. Wait for me."

What can I do but nod?

I flee back to the queen's rooms before anyone can
notice me. Already I fear that one of the men will report
they found Raleigh drinking alone in the cellars. Even if
this is his wine he gave to the queen, will she take kindly
to him helping himself like this?

Unable to take the anxiety, I keep myself busy. I
volunteer to help Lady Russell with fetching the oils for
her majesty's bath. Then I help with the arduous task of
packing away her dresses, carefully ensuring they are
wrapped in parchment and sprigs of dried lavender. The
queen has roomfuls of gowns ready to be worn. There are
rumours she never wears the same dress twice and this is
mostly true. As I return some of these dresses to her
wardrobes, I walk past several gowns too fine to be folded
away. They lie draped on hangers and covered in gauze

to keep dust away. At last count she has amassed over a thousand fine dresses, but after this latest victory more will come. Loyal subjects will wish to shower her with gifts to show their gratitude. Soon she will need to give away some of these fine garments or build new wardrobe rooms.

Back in her rooms I help Blanche Parry mix the queen's face powder. A new batch must be made every day. Fear of poisoning is too great to buy the cream from a merchant or leave it lying around. The men around the queen are scrupulous in caring for her safety. Indeed, it is thanks to the men she has carefully selected to serve her that she is alive today.

As we help the queen dress, she mentions that Leicester has excused himself. Blanche pauses applying her makeup to give the queen's thin hand a gentle squeeze. The queen's old nursemaid knows her charge well.

Indeed, the cheer has gone from the queen. As she watches a choir perform a song for her, she never smiles once. She is hiding behind a veil that will only lift when Leicester returns.

He does not and never will.

In his first letter he says he will travel to the country to Kenninghall to rest and recover after the stress of the last few days.

The celebrations go on without him. His stepson proves himself an adept replacement, but even he cannot improve the queen's increasingly dark moods.

Then a rider arrives at Whitehall before evening. He

is pale and does not linger for a reward. He hands his message off to Essex and rides away.

Cecil comes to the queen's room. We try to bar him as she is changing, but in the face of his sombre blank stare we allow him through.

I listen at the door, my heart wrenching as the queen hears the news she has feared was coming for days. Her cries echo through her apartments. We set to work emptying her rooms of visitors and guests. No one must hear her sobs. They cannot report back to their masters that the queen collapsed upon hearing that her friend of old has died. We are part of the propaganda machine that has made her appear larger than life. Human emotions should be beyond her.

It becomes harder to keep the secret as she locks herself in her bedchamber. She doesn't allow anyone inside, not even Blanche Parry, who begs her.

The councillors debate in her presence chamber if picking the lock would be acceptable. Meanwhile, we resort to tempting her out with food and water.

Days later, Cecil, Walsingham, and the Lord Treasurer arrive at her door with a troop of locksmiths. They force the door open and the councillors eventually emerge with the queen.

She is thin and gaunt, but otherwise there is no evidence of her sorrow. She dines in private with her closest companions. I am among those chosen to serve her. As I take a trencher of venison from a servant, Cecil beckons me to him.

I approach with a slight bow of my head to show respect as he makes a great show of studying the meat.

"Ply her with food and drink. Don't let her plate be empty. Make sure the kitchen is bringing up her favourites."

I nod and move away.

For a few days we tiptoe around the queen, taking special care not to do anything that would upset her. At last she snaps.

"Enough of this. Am I an invalid that you treat me so?"

Blanche Parry lets out one of her cackling laughs. "They fear you will lock yourself away again, Your Grace."

"As well I should," the queen says, waving her hands over us. "Enough. I have mourned for the loss of a dear friend. It is done now. Let's have some music, some noise. I tire of this quiet." A moment later, she begins pacing the room restlessly. "Send for Walsingham. I want a full report of what I have missed."

Months go by and I find I must make do with secret smiles and nods from Raleigh. Sometimes he partners me in dances or during pageants, but these are few and far between.

During the grand celebrations for Ascension Day in November, I steal a kiss and tell him I grow impatient with waiting. Does he not understand how I suffer?

I begin to doubt him and ask the queen for permission to visit my brother for Christmas to be there for his first child's christening.

I find Arthur in his London house, cooing over his daughter's cradle.

"I hope the roads were good," he says, looking away for only a second.

"They were," I say. "I am glad to have arrived before supper is served. How is the little darling? You seem enamoured with her already."

"As every father should be," he says and steps back so I might see my first niece.

She is a few weeks old, but her cheeks are already plump and she has a clear complexion.

"She has her mother's dark hair. Ann is disappointed. She hoped her daughter would inherit our family's colouring."

I scoff and wave it away. "She's perfect just as she is."

I place a finger on her cheek. Her attention snaps from her father to me, her little mouth scrunches up, and she begins to cry.

The wet nurse rushes forward and takes her to go feed her. I watch the pair of them go with a frown.

My brother, guessing my thought, puts a hand on my shoulders. "She is just hungry or needs changing. Don't take it personally."

"I've never had luck with children or babes. It doesn't matter."

"It must still sting your ego."

I shrug him off for the joke and he smiles. "Well, go

see Ann. She's eager to leave her rooms, though the priests say she must stay in confinement another week."

I spend a lovely week at my brother's house. The intimate smaller setting is a breath of fresh air from the often stilted manner of the court. I am due to leave the day after Elizabeth's christening. The queen, hearing the babe was named after her, sends a small bracelet of thin gold as a present but sadly does not offer to stand as godparent.

"Don't fret," I say, but Lady Ann doesn't smile. "She has hundreds of godchildren. She does not dote on all of them. Find someone that will love and shower little Lizzy with gifts."

The morning I am due to leave, a maid knocks on my door and presents an unsealed letter to me. As I stare at it there's a ringing in my ears. I take a deep breath to steady myself before reaching out for it.

"Who's it from?" I ask in what I hope is my most nonchalant voice.

"A gentleman brought it. Said his name was Master Gilbert. From the court, I reckon," she says.

"Hmm. Thank you." I open the letter and skim the contents, ignoring the elation threatening to spew forth. "The queen has urged me to hurry my departure. Can you inform my brother?"

She curtsies and leaves me in the doorway. Carefully, I close the door behind me. Alone from prying eyes I reread the letter.

Inn of the Dragonhead. Today at noon. Wait for me but leave if I am not there within the hour. —W

No one suspects me as I leave my brother's house early with a manservant to escort me. By barge I am rolled up the Thames, my heart beating in time with the drums that keep the rowers steady. It shall fail and give out if I am delayed a second longer.

At the quayside I dismiss the manservant and then head toward the sprawling castle. However, before I am through the gates I double back and walk through the city, my cloak pulled around me tightly as I go.

How I reach the Inn of the Dragonhead I do not know, but he is there.

I see the joy spring into his eyes at the sight of me.

He hurries me inside, but instead of remaining we leave out the back way. My hand is in his, but in the excitement I follow without question. We stop in front of an unmarked door above a milliner's shop. Raleigh pulls out a thin key from his breast pocket and opens the door for me. My eyebrow arches up in question, but he motions with his head for me to climb up the steps.

Up I go. The stucco white walls are plain but freshly painted. The steps might be uneven but are sturdy and don't creak.

The landing leads to a small room, random pieces of furniture scattered about. The windows with their blinds drawn create an ominous effect.

I frown as I turn back to see he has come up the steps, a spring in his step.

"What is this?"

He grins. "Our secret." He laughs, seeing how confused I still am. "This is mine. I rented the rooms. I know it's not much now, but I will make sure that we have everything needful."

"For what?" I interrupt him. "Are you expecting me to live here?" Already the room feels like it's closing in on me.

Raleigh scratches the back of his head as if he wasn't expecting this sort of reaction from me. "I thought we might on occasion meet here so we may be together in private without fear of discovery."

My lips part, but words are lost to me. "You wish to keep me here as your shameful secret? A mistress you can bed whenever you please?"

He has the decency to wince at my crass words.

I nearly turn to go, but instead I cross my arms in front of me, waiting for him to explain.

"I wish I could kiss you openly and proclaim my love for you to the world. Whether or not we married, I have many enemies who would use this against me. The queen would be jealous and I would lose her favour."

I shrug as if I don't care.

"It's not only me I am thinking of but you. Are you truly ready to leave court behind and go be a wife in the country? Do you even wish to marry me?"

My lips purse into two thin lines, but I don't contradict him. I am torn and cannot answer that even in my daydreams I have not settled on anything beyond wishing for the heated touching and kissing that goes on between the two of us to continue. The thought of leaving my treasured position at court tips the scales.

"I do not agree to be your whore."

"Never."

"Nor your mistress."

The corners of his lips twitch as if he's fighting back a smile. "What would you like to call yourself then? You don't want to be my wife, yet your hunger for me is insatiable."

I gape at him, narrowing my eyes. "We can be friends, Sir."

He approaches me with slow deliberate movements. I let him. When he presses himself against me, his next words come out as a harsh breath against my ear that leaves me breathing hard.

"Only friends?"

Like the consummate liar I am, I nod.

"Shall we test out the truth of your words?" His hand captures my chin and forces me to look up at him. Even if I wanted to, I cannot avoid his searing gaze. My eyes flutter, half closing from the intensity of our closeness.

"Answer me," he commands.

I let out a moan and can only nod.

He leans closer, his lips grazing the middle of my neck. "Say it."

I close my eyes, my stubborn pride getting the better of my attraction to him. But as he pulls away I find I am desperate to keep him near me.

"Yes. I want you."

He leads me through the door to the bedroom beyond. The feather mattress is covered in fresh linen and plush blankets.

He knew this rendezvous would lead to this. He was

prepared. I cannot fault him. Anger and shame melt away under his delicate touch. I never want this moment to end.

After, as I lie curled up against him, I sigh, content as a well-fed lioness.

"I take it you are pleased with my performance."

I wiggle in his arms at his crude talk.

"Peace, Bess. Otherwise I might have to start kissing you again."

Though I let out a yelp, the thought appeals to me. I have to force myself to stop. We have to talk. There's no way we can go on like this indefinitely.

I look over my shoulder to find him with his eyes closed and his breathing settling into an easy rhythm. The thought of sleeping beside him is appealing and far less complicated than talking right now.

He cracks one eye open and it's too late to turn back now.

"I want to be your love. That means no other women unless we end things between us."

He pinches the skin above my hip. "Why would we ever end things between us?"

I smile. "If the earth opens up and swallows me whole, then I give you permission to find comfort elsewhere."

"Generous of you."

"Or when I tire of you," I add.

Suddenly he's on top of me, straddling me. "Tire of me? Mademoiselle, please. I thought we laid that matter to rest."

I roll my hips and hide a smile at the groan I extract from him. If this was a battle of wills, we'd both lose.

"Get off, this is serious," I say and he reluctantly obeys. "What do you want?" My heart aches even as I ask the question. Of course I should have known the great poet would have a ready answer for me.

"What else?" He regards me with those enviously green eyes of his. "You."

Delighted, I pull him toward me once more but hesitate at the last moment. "And if there is a child?"

"Why then, I suppose you shall have to say yes."

"To what?"

"Marrying me." His lazy drawl is enough to make me come undone.

I hum with pleasure but don't deny the practicality. He's right. I would say yes and not entirely because I would have been forced to.

In years to come, I will question whether I made the right choice, but at the moment I cannot imagine living without him. I see now why lust is one of the seven deadly sins. Even these stolen moments alone are worth risking God's retribution.

We return separately to court before nightfall, evidence of our dealings hidden away behind my veneer of cold serenity.

As a gift for the new year the queen is generous with all her ladies. I receive a purple kirtle cut in the French style, embroidered with black satin thread and trimmed with velvet. It's a sumptuous gift. I already imagine myself pairing it with my black sleeves slashed to allow white sleeves to poke through. It's cut low, leaving little to the imagination.

When I wear it at the next feast I catch the attention of many men, who follow me as I dance with a familiar hunger in their eyes. I grin at the frown on Raleigh's face as I accept partner after partner. He doesn't know, but every smile, every laugh is for him.

The following day as we ride out to hunt with the queen, he pulls me aside.

"Your horse has foundered, Lady Bess," he says, loud enough should anyone hear. "I shall stay with you until someone can be brought to assist you."

"Can you not offer me your own mount?" I tease, pressing my body against his coquettishly as he helps me from the saddle. "He is not the sort of beast I am used to riding, but he will do."

I clasp my hands over my mouth to smother a laugh that threatens to be heard by everyone in England at Raleigh's thunderous expression.

He leads me further into the glen, leading our horses by their reins.

I wait for him to tie up the horses, my back leaning against a tree. I am already removing my gloves as he approaches.

"We didn't get a chance to discuss my expectations," he says, using his body and arms deliberately to cage me against the tree. My chest is heaving at his closeness, heat pooling deliciously in the pit of my stomach.

I study the curve of Raleigh's lips. Of its own accord my tongue flicks out, moistening my lower lip.

"Oh?" I'm already lost in the haze of desire he incites.

"I cannot tolerate you taking other lovers or showering others with your affection. If I remain yours, you must pledge yourself to me as well."

"Until the earth swallows you whole?"

"Yes, until then."

"Very well, I agree to the terms of your contract." He's pressing into me. My eyes spark with mischief. "How shall we place a seal on this—contract?"

"I can think of a few ways." The intensity in his eyes alone is enough to make my toes curl in delight.

CHAPTER 8

WINTER 1589 - AUTUMN 1591

Perhaps it was only my imagination or my previous blindness that made me blind to what was going on right in front of me. Everywhere I turn couples sneak off for stolen moments here and there. The queen has forbidden the marriage of one of her ladies, but that doesn't stop the lady in question from sneaking off with a gentleman usher when she should be at prayer.

I live in secret fear that Raleigh and I will be discovered. This fear only abates with time. Likewise, my fear of conceiving a child.

I dare not take any potions or keep anything in my room. It would inevitably be discovered, especially the potion was to make me ill. The queen loathes physicians and their tinctures. She takes this hatred seriously and is not above banishing her own ladies for taking them.

Raleigh claims to take precautions, but I begin to suspect I might be barren. If it means this pleasure between us can go on indefinitely, then I am resigned.

Marriage is something I regard as an impossibility. Raleigh grows in the queen's esteem and so does his wealth. He has become a catch and he's a calculating sort of man. I am fully aware that if he ever chooses to marry it would be a rich heiress, who could enhance his position. Not to mention someone the queen would approve of.

It might have hurt more if I wasn't so assured of his desire for me.

We slip away to be together while the court is hunting. For once we simply sit side by side watching a small stream trickle by.

Feeling nostalgic I say, "do you remember the first time we spoke? You had come across me stuck in the water."

He chuckles removing his hat. "How could I forget? I thought you were going to have my head for rescuing you."

"I was embarrassed and I didn't know you as I do now." I find myself resting my head against the padding of his sleeves. If I closed my eyes now I could doze away in an instant. Instead, I study a pair of dragonflies skimming the surface of the water.

"You would never have guessed how concerned I was for you."

"I remember you didn't hesitate from carrying me off on your horse against my will."

"You make me sound like a raiding barbarian come to steal you away."

Glancing up, I study his far-off expression. "What are you thinking of?"

"I am returning home to the country this summer while the queen goes on progress."

"So we shall be separated." My shoulders slump.

His arm snakes itself around me. I feel his warm reassuring hold on me. "It will be longer than that, I'm afraid."

A lump has made its way into my throat. "Oh?"

"Afraid so. I will be taking to the sea once more. It was never my plan to dally in England for long."

"I see." Lowering my head I try to get a hold of my emotions. I hadn't expected to miss him so keenly.

"I wish I could take you with me." His hand tilts my chin up so he can study me. "I yearn for you already."

"But not enough to stay."

In answer, his lips brush against my own.

There is no future with him but despite that I can't let him go either.

With the summer comes the plague and those who can hurry out of the city. Raleigh's duties take him home to the country while I travel with the queen's reduced court as she goes on progress visiting the great houses of the land.

The bliss and tranquillity in the kingdom after the defeat of the Spanish cannot last forever.

Little more than a year passes before bad news after

bad news begins to taint the queen's mood. This seems to coincide with bad weather and luck for me.

First, Blanche Parry passes away. The old lady, brittle as paper, succumbs at last to old age. The queen cannot be comforted, even by the fact that she died in peace during the night.

Elizabeth orders the court to go into mourning and has her buried with pomp due to a lady of far greater rank in Bacton. To compound the love she felt for Blanche, she sends for the dress she wore for the Armada portrait.

I watch mutely as the queen examines it for a brief moment before saying that the silk fabric with its embroidery of silver and gold thread should be given to the church where Blanche is buried. The gown is worth a fortune. Cecil warns that the church may pawn off the silk and suggests Elizabeth make a gift of money instead.

The queen fixes him with a look that silences him forever on the subject.

A string of deaths follow: men close to Elizabeth who have served her from her youth, the Earl of Warwick, and then perhaps worst of all, Sir Francis Walsingham. The queen is distraught over his loss, but Cecil is even more so. Walsingham's spy network was one of the best in the world. He was the first line of defence against plots at home and abroad.

By summer the dark cloud hanging over the country lifts.

Everyone is in a jovial mood, but I find it hard to join in the fun. Raleigh has left to try to thwart the Spanish, and I miss his company more than I ought to.

"Why so glum?" Katherine Bridges says to me as she comes to help pin my hair into place.

"Homesick," I say, having prepared my answer a long time ago. "The court is usually so merry, but..."

"I understand," she says, scrunching up her nose. "We've had nothing to do but attend funerals. God rest their souls." She adds the last part as an afterthought. "However, if you are looking for some amusement, I might just have the thing for you."

My interest is piqued. "What?"

"Not here," she whispers, looking right and left at the other ladies busy with their toilets. "But I'll bring it to you tonight."

"It" happens to be a translation of an Italian work. It is printed on cheap parchment but appears to be well thumbed. The title, *Orlando Furioso*, is smudged. I vaguely recall hearing of this, but from what I remember it was an Italian poem.

"Sir John Harington translated it," Katherine whispers.

"Or so he claims."

She looks surprised at my insinuation that a man could lie. I look at her with compassion. She is still young, barely twenty this fall, and perhaps not wise to the ways of the world.

"There's no author's name on this. He could have had one of his lackeys do the translation or stolen it from some other poor soul." Her face falls and I see she is eyeing the paper as if regretting showing me. "Or you are correct and he did write it. I was just speculating."

Her smile is back. I wince at how easy it is to turn her. She would be easy prey for any villain.

"I appreciate you sharing this with me," I continue. "Regardless of the author, I will enjoy it."

She grins. "I'm sure you will. Don't let the others see it."

"Hasn't it been circulating around?" I hide my exasperation and force myself to smile. "But I promise I will keep it secret."

I only take it out to read in the evenings before we all retire to bed. The turns of phrase and prose are beautiful. The subject matter is—lewd, to put it bluntly, often times veering off into being crude. I can now believe that the likes of John Harington wrote this. He has skill, that much is undeniable, but he lacks tact or a natural instinct when it comes to romance. Though perhaps being shocking was his intention all along.

I return the pamphlet and put it out of my mind until one morning the queen comes stomping out of her bedchamber. Elizabeth Russell is sobbing in the chamber beyond. What did she do?

The queen looks around at us as if we have greatly disappointed her. There's a pang in my chest as her gaze passes over me. I want to disappear within myself.

She flourishes a parchment before casting it down at her feet. "Who wrote this filth?"

My throat clenches as I recognise it at once.

None of us are fool enough to answer her.

"You are my maids-in-waiting. Your decorum is a reflection of me. I don't want it whispered around Chris-

THE PIRATE LORD'S WIFE

tendom that I allow untoward behaviour or, God forbid, that I encourage it. Tell me who the author is or I will banish you all from court."

This isn't an empty threat.

I grip the armrest of my seat for strength. The answer is ready to come spilling out, but another lady blushes and admits that she believes Sir John Harington is the translator.

The queen's fury descends upon her. But she is fair and summons Harington to the presence chamber. This will be a rather public dressing down, and as we file in I am filled with dread and fear that, beyond embarrassment, the queen will have us questioned and arrested. It takes all my strength to steady myself and keep my expression detached. There are several supplicants waiting in the presence chamber, but seeing the queen's fury, none dare approach her.

I know what it must have cost them to gain access to this inner sanctum. Bribes come my way just to put a kind word in the queen's ear or one of her councillors' so that they might have the chance to see the queen. All power flows from the queen. Even those who dislike her or disapprove of the idea of a woman on the throne swallow down their feelings and approach the queen with a gracious smile.

At last Harington appears, his steps stilted as he approaches the throne. His eyes keep darting around the room searching for assistance or escape. It's clear he's been warned that he's in trouble, but if he were in any doubt the queen's blazing expression would confirm his worst fears.

I watch as he falls into a deep bow and stays down. We wait for her to invite him to rise, but she does not. Harington remains frozen in place, his eyes glued to the floor as the queen stands and takes slow studied steps down from the dais.

The pamphlet is in her hand now and she raises it above her head. I wince as I watch her hand come sailing down. There's a resounding *thwack* as the paper hits him on the head.

"Your Majesty," he breathes out as if he has been punched in the gut.

"Explain yourself."

He raises his head, but she is quick to correct him. "I didn't give you permission to rise."

Harington clears his throat and starts again. "Your Majesty, forgive your servant for his trespasses. I never meant to anger you with my translations."

"You know of the chaste household I run. Why would you then print such a rude paper and on top of that let it circulate among my very own ladies?"

He opens and closes his mouth several times. I look away, unable to bear watching this embarrassing display. The answer is obvious—he circulated it because it was popular and sought after. The queen is baiting him into stepping into the fire. "I wasn't thinking, Your Grace. Forgive me. I thought it was a jest. I should have realised how much this would upset you."

"Not just me," she quips. "You've brought some of

my ladies to tears. You young men are all the same." She shakes her head, but the edge of her anger is gone. "You may rise."

He does so, his knees visibly trembling as she returns to her throne.

Elizabeth's eyes travel from the paper in her hand to her godson's fear-stricken face.

"Since you have such a flair for translation and apparently have so much free time on your hands, why don't I assign you a more appropriate task?"

"I would be honoured, Your Majesty," he says.

"You know of Ariosto's work?"

Harington shifts from one leg to another. "Yes, Your Majesty."

"Good. You are not to come into my presence or even be seen at court until you have finished translating his entire work."

He is gaping at her but knows better than to protest. I haven't read Ariosto myself, but I know there are several volumes that would surely take months to complete. This is no small task she set him.

He bows and thanks her, apologising again.

The queen waves him off. Once he has left, she turns to us and the room at large. "Let this be an example to all of you. I don't tolerate improper behaviour."

There's a sharp pain in my chest as though she has grabbed my heart and squeezed. What would she do if she ever discovered my dealings with Raleigh?

~

Harington is not the last person to be reprimanded for bad behaviour. The queen's new favourite, it is revealed, has married in secret. As an earl it is required he ask permission before marrying. The queen could overlook this if it wasn't for his choice.

Frances Walsingham, the penniless daughter of her old spymaster and widow of Philip Sidney, is hardly worthy of marriage to an earl. At least that is what the queen claims.

She toys with the idea of imprisoning Essex. They have a few days of tempestuous fights. Her other ladies and I are caught in the crossfire of their arguments. When Essex raises his voice, he oversteps the rules of decorum, yet the queen doesn't banish him. She simply shouts louder.

When he threatens to leave court and never return, she retreats to her bedchamber.

I am amazed watching the two of them. There is so much affection and hate all wrapped up in this exchange. He resents her power, yet craves the homage she doles out. Only with her approval can he reach his aspirations. His appetite, like Leicester in his youth, is endless. As for the queen, it is clear that she finds him handsome and his strong personality presents a welcome change for her. However, she is still queen and she doesn't want him to forget it.

He stomps off and makes a great show of preparing to leave court. She summons him back to her rooms, where again he apologises.

His penance is not done, but she invites him to join

her on a walk in the gardens. Essex's victory is incomplete because the queen swears that she will never receive his wife at court.

Raleigh is back in time to witness this exchange. Our eyes meet across the room, though we quickly look away.

Two days later we meet in secret. After we have sated our baser appetites, I draw him into conversation.

"The queen is on high alert for any bad behaviour. I worry that her patience will wear thin and if we are discovered then she will decide to punish us harshly just to be an example."

Raleigh hushes me.

"But what shall we do?"

He kisses the back of my neck, that delicate area that sends shivers down my spine. "Deny. Deny. Deny," he says like a prayer as he continues his gentle caresses.

"You'd deny me?" Though the delights of his touch are getting harder to ignore, I turn around so we are face-to-face. He sighs, seeing that I will not be put off.

"I would expect you to deny me as well," he says. His expression is serious, but his words hurt me. Does this all mean nothing to him? The time apart had been difficult for me.

"How could I?" I look down to hide the tears threatening to spill from my eyes.

He tilts my chin up to face him. "Sweetheart, don't be like this. If it is a matter of your safety, then yes, I will deny everything. It doesn't mean you don't haunt my dreams when I am away from you."

Shy as a colt, I dare to smile. "But what if I were to conceive?"

"We shall cross that threshold when we get there," he says, using his thumb to brush away the tears that I am unable to hold back.

I hug my knees and nod. "I should go on to my brother's house. He is expecting me."

He doesn't protest. Our time together is always like this: brief and succinct. We don't have time to dawdle over words and conversations. I worry he is pleased to have me as his mistress. Maybe he's even pleased that I am barren. Then I scold myself for being so distrustful. If I suspect him of something foul, then why can't I stay away? Is this some spell he has cast over me?

We continue on like this, meeting in secret, exchanging notes and little gifts. Months slip away and all of a sudden another year has passed us by.

I am happy with the way things are. Thrilled with his attention and with my growing responsibilities as a maid of honour. When Raleigh is not at court attending the queen, he is at Durham House planning his next expedition. Beyond our love play I know this is where his true passion lies and I cannot fault him for it. Instead, I respect him for avoiding being consumed by love and lust as I am constantly on the verge of being. King Henry of France, the first Protestant French king, is facing a civil war. His ambassadors scurry around the queen like flies attracted to honey. They urge her to help them, but finances are tight, and having come out unscathed after the war with Spain, she is unwilling to commit English soldiers.

"Do you think she should?" I ask Raleigh one evening. By all accounts I should be at my brother's London house, celebrating the birth of a second daughter, this one named Anne.

"Go to war?" He shakes his head. "No, I am not like Essex."

I wrap my arms around his neck, looking over his shoulder at the letter he is penning with so much thought. I see it is a list of items for his voyage.

"You'd make a handsome general."

"Would I?" He looks up at me, grinning. "Is that why you wish for war? To see me strut about in armour?"

I laugh. "It has crossed my mind."

He rolls his eyes. "Perhaps you wish to be rid of me. My dying in battle would suit you."

"That is a cruel thing to say." I am watching him carefully now. I catch a strange look flick across his face. It's gone in a moment before I put my finger on it. "I could never imagine you doing something as boring as perishing in battle." I twirl my finger around a lock of his hair. These days he has let his hair grow long and unruly.

This time his flinch is unmistakable. I pull away and slip on the lined robe.

When I turn back around I find him watching me with those impervious green eyes of his. "We've been at this game for over three years now—"

"And you tire of it?" I interrupt him, ignoring the chill spreading over me that is so acute I pray I won't convulse into a fit.

His eyes darken. "No."

My relief is palatable. "Good," I say, hazarding a grin. "Then what has you in such a dark mood?"

"You wish us to continue on like this indefinitely?" He keeps his tone casual, but I sense a trap. I don't know what to say. Is he testing me?

"I love you."

"You didn't answer the question."

"I don't know what you want me to say."

"The truth."

My own anger rises to the surface. What more could he want from me? I am risking everything just to be with him. If he wanted—more—why did he not ask? Out of stubbornness I wait for him to continue the conversation, but he returns to his work.

We part for the first time on bad terms.

I ignore his next note. Partly out of pettiness, but partly out of an illness that has seized me.

The fish we are served on Friday tastes off, and I spend the evening sweating and feverish. I take several days to recover. The queen orders a private room prepared for me so I might convalesce in quiet. Of course this is not for my benefit alone. I am being isolated from spreading my sickness to everyone else.

I sleep the days away and sip hot broth, the only thing I can stomach.

A knock at my chamber door makes my heart skip a

beat. I begin to hope it is Raleigh and rush to open the door myself.

I find Arthur standing there in his riding clothes.

"Sister, should you not be in bed?"

"Yes, but I heard the knock."

"Where's your maid?" He frowns. "Shouldn't she be at your side?"

"I sent her to get some bread and porridge from the kitchen," I say before inviting him inside.

He looks around the room, frowning at the scent of stale air and illness. Arthur takes a seat by the fire and I return to my bed, feeling the dizziness returning.

"Why are you here? Besides to check in on your favourite sister?"

"The queen has called a parliament. We are to discuss sending troops to France. Matters are growing dire there. The Spanish have thrown their support behind the Catholic rival for the French throne."

I let out a hiss of disapproval. All-out war again. I regret not meeting with Raleigh more than ever.

"There is other news," he begins. Then, seeing my face, he rushes to reassure me. "We are all well. Our sister, Mary, is to be married."

I blink in shock. "Little Mary?"

"She's eighteen, and next spring she will turn nineteen. He's of an age with her and a good match. Henry is the son of Sir Andrew Philips. Remember the one who owns that little manor farm neighbouring our land? She will be settled quite close to Coughton."

My eyebrow shoots up. "Well, that will be lovely. I hope she will be very happy."

"Yes." He lets out a sigh. "She broke a storm over my head when she heard the news."

"Why? She doesn't want to marry him?" My heart goes out to her. It's been years since I have seen her, but I wouldn't wish her to be unhappy.

"She thought he was too lowly born for her," Arthur scoffs, kicking his boot. "She wanted to come to court and find an earl or a duke to marry." He turns to face me, his eyes twinkling with amusement. "I tried to tell her you haven't exactly had much luck on that front, and she swore she would do a better job and wouldn't act like a nun."

I nearly choke. If only my family knew. "So what happened to make the match go ahead?"

"I invited the prospective groom and his father to dine with us. Low and behold, our sister had a sudden change of heart after that."

"Ah," I say with a knowing grin. "So he's handsome."

"I suppose he is."

"Well, I wish them every joy. He is a good man, is he not?"

"As far as I know." He pauses, seeing the look of distaste that crosses my face. "Don't look at me like that. I talked to him, inquired after him and his family. He is a serious hardworking man."

I hum but trust he did his due diligence.

~

I recover enough over the next few days to return to my duties. My stomach is still uneasy and I cannot stand the smell of fish anymore.

As November approaches, the opportunity for me to speak to Raleigh diminishes. Everyone is on edge and alert, but also because he has been consumed with plans for another voyage.

In apology he sends me a rose pin. The solid gold piece is studded with delicate emeralds. A beautiful piece, yet one that is unlikely to draw attention.

As I dance in the pageant for Ascension Day, I pin it to my hair. I feel his piercing gaze on me as I twirl past him, knowing he will move mountains to see me again.

My movements become emboldened and I dare look back to him with a sultry smile he's sure not to miss before I turn back to the dance.

Two days later I agree to meet him. My cheeks are flushed from the biting wind as he helps me remove my cloak.

"It's been too long." He wraps his arms around me in a tight embrace. I hear him breathing in deep.

I agree and pull him toward what I now regard as our bed.

After we both take our pleasure in each other, we lie side by side gazing into each other's faces.

"I'm sorry we have missed so much time."

"It's in the past. After all this time, it's a miracle we haven't argued more often."

I frown. "It's rather hard to argue if we hardly talk."

He's begun trailing his fingertips over my smooth flesh.

I do my best to ignore my delight at his touch. "I forgot what we even fought about."

"I did too," he says, reassuring me. Then he stops, his hand resting lightly on my stomach. "Dearest, I do believe you are growing plump."

"That's surprising. I haven't had much of an appetite."

He continues his slow lingering strokes.

But after a moment I shoot up. My heart is racing.

"What is it?"

I rack my brain, trying to remember the last time I bled. It's been at least three months. My mouth is dry and I let out an audible gasp.

He's up now too. "Are you sick? What is wrong?"

"No. My—I might be with child."

I watch his eyes go wide in genuine surprise. "We haven't seen each other in a month..."

"Are you accusing me of something?" I glare at him.

"No, it's just that maybe with your recent sickness it's thrown things off."

If this weren't so serious, I'd be amused by the awkward way he stumbles over his words. Slowly, I shake my head.

"It's been three months and maybe a bit longer since I bled."

There's a sharp intake of breath from him as he regards me. "Should we send for a doctor?"

"Do we dare?"

He shakes his head.

I bite my knuckles to keep myself from crying out. He wraps his arms around me and holds me tight. Then, as my sobs begin to stop, he starts stroking my hair.

"We knew this was a possibility...I will take care of you. Both of you."

I will myself to wake up from this dream. No, nightmare. After so many years I am not prepared for the magnitude.

Pulling away, I wipe my tears. "I-I'm not even sure. We will wait and see if the child quickens. I will speak to my brother."

Raleigh listens to me rambling off things I plan on doing. "And where is the father of your child in all of this planning?"

From the corner of my eye I regard him. A deep yearning from within me pushes aside my pride and I confess in a soft whisper, "I hoped you might marry me."

I hate how weak and pleading that sounds, but his mask falls away to show pure relief on his face. He tilts my head up and kisses me on the lips. "I always told you I would—if you wished me to."

"I thought you might not wish to."

He laughs. "You were the one who was so callous and distant about our relationship. I felt like you would banish me from your bed at any moment."

Under normal circumstances I would rage at him. But with my tears and anger spent I am left shaking my head before I playfully nudge him. "We clearly have a lot to talk about."

It's decided we shall conceal the pregnancy and marriage. Running afoul of the queen at this time would be bad for the both of us. Raleigh will find a priest and marry me in a private ceremony. Being able to move around without suspicion, he will visit my brother at Coughton.

"If this expedition is successful, then I will return to England with riches beyond the queen's dreams. She will forgive me anything then." He kisses my brow.

"Will you return before the baby is born?" I'm afraid to ask what will happen if he does not.

"Fear not," he says. "I will speak to your brother. He will conceal you and the babe at his home. There can always be some excuse."

CHAPTER 9

WINTER 1592 - SUMMER 1592

U sing my illness as an excuse, I do my best to play up my symptoms. I am seen to be eating very little yet complaining of bloating in my stomach.

When a concerned Catherine Howard approaches me, I reassure her I have seen a physician.

"The queen would understand if you needed time to recover," she says. There's something about her choice of words that strikes me as odd, but she smiles and pats my back in soothing circles. I close my eyes for a moment. My back has been aching, yet I haven't dared tell anyone.

"I will write to my brother and see if I may stay with him for a time."

"That may be best," Catherine says. Then she takes a long pause. "You know you could confide in me if you ever needed a friend, don't you?"

My body stiffens, but I force myself to smile. "Thank you, that's very kind. I will be sure to keep it in mind."

I do write to my brother. I receive a curt reply from

my sister-in-law saying they will be ready to receive me in February and to let her know if I shall be needing an escort. Though I am taken aback by this, my attention is diverted by the amount of skill it takes to hide my growing belly. But as Raleigh said to me all those nights ago, deny, deny, deny.

After a time no one comments on my growing girth, and I begin to hope Raleigh and I will be able to pull this off.

In February, I am taken to my brother's house by horseback. I dare not request a litter. I only pray that this will not hurt the baby in some way. We go slowly, but at last in the distance I can make out Coughton Court. I could cry with relief at safety being in arm's reach.

My brother waits for me on the steps. It takes me only a second to register his stony expression. My heart aches and I cannot stop the tears from streaming down my face. How will I take his disapproval? He softens as a groom holds my horse steady and another helps me from the saddle.

My legs wobble, and that is when Arthur steps forward, offering me his arm. He doesn't say a word of greeting. But at least that look of pure disappointment is gone.

In the entranceway behind the double door, I am surprised to find Raleigh there.

I fly to his open arms and he kisses me, placing a hand on my belly. "Are you both well?"

I nod. "As good as can be." I sneak a glance over my

THE PIRATE LORD'S WIFE

shoulder. My brother has his back turned to us, examining the woodwork on his doorway.

"He will come round. He loves you," Raleigh whispers to me. "Now I must flee back to London before I am missed. Remember, anything you might hear, you must trust our love." He takes my hand and places it over his heart. "We must play our cards right."

"Even if we must deny everything?"

"Especially that. Fare thee well, my beloved wife."

"I love you," I say simply, and then he leaves me alone in the company of a brother who cannot look me in the eye. Never once since my affair with Raleigh began have I felt such shame as potent as this.

"Lady Ann is in her presence chamber, sewing with her women. You may join her. She has taken care of assigning you rooms and the like."

Taking a step toward him, I say, "Arthur, I'm sorry. For not telling you." I clear my throat. "How could I? But I was compelled by love. I cannot live without him."

"You may have to now."

I am not expecting the cold snap of his voice. It knocks the wind out of me. "What do you mean?"

"You cannot return to court. What will you do after the baby is born? Will he publicly declare you as his wife?"

"We—" I stop myself from laying our plans out to him. Even if I did, it's clear he would take it badly. "Very well. Be angry with me, but know that I still appreciate all that you do for me."

He takes a step forward. "Bess, what choice did I

have? How could I let you be publicly shamed? I hoped you'd be happy with your work at court or find some other employment. I even hoped you might start a family of your own. You lied to me and swore there was nothing between you and Raleigh. Like a fool I trusted you."

"At the time that hadn't been a lie and I found happiness." A protective hand goes to my belly.

He shakes his head incredulously. "He's made you his whore and tucked you away in the country to have his child. Our family will bear the brunt of the shame and the expense. I am only grateful that your sister's wedding has already gone ahead. Who will want to associate with us now when news of this gets out? Mark my words, it will displease the queen."

"She might not find out. No one needs to know. Raleigh loves me. I wanted to be happy—"

"Are you happy now?"

I'm too busy wiping away my tears to answer.

"The marriage contract I've signed—you will get a pittance. He's a man of great fortune, and despite his reputation, under normal circumstances I would have welcomed him as my brother-in-law. Listen to me, Bess. Not only has he ruined you and then married you in secret, but he has only settled two hundred pounds per annum on you. If he were to die, that would be the only thing you are entitled to. If he cared about you, he would not lay aside such a small sum."

"He's a g-good man," I struggle to say. "Don't say such horrid things. I know about the money. He is putting his fortune into his colony in America. There are costs—"

He interrupts me with a loud barking laugh. "Two hundred pounds is not enough for you and your child. Does he care more about the colony than you?" I get a respite from his tirade only long enough for him to take another breath. "Are you even sure it was a proper priest? Let me guess, he only wanted to marry you after you were pregnant. Tell me I'm wrong. Tell me what I'm missing."

"Arthur!" On the stairs, his wife, who is visibly pregnant as well, is plodding down the steps. She must have heard our loud voices. All of Coughton must have.

My cheeks burn red, but I don't look away.

Lady Ann embraces me and glares at my brother, who is trying to get a hold of his temper.

"She should be resting after such a long journey. How can you yell at a woman in her condition? Come with me Bess. I'll take you to the chamber I prepared for you." Lady Ann takes me by the hand and leads me away.

I'm halfway up the stairs before I turn around and call down, "I have proof of the wedding ceremony. The contract between us is signed and sealed. If this doesn't make a marriage, what does? You can be reassured in that respect at least."

He avoids making eye contact with me.

Coughton used to have such pleasant memories for me, but now they are tainted. I cannot officially go into confinement, but I keep to my rooms as much as possible.

There's a plush bed, covered with furs and heavy blankets to keep me warm. I have a midwife to attend me and a maidservant to help me with everything else.

Once or twice I venture to my sister-in-law's rooms, but I don't know the women she has around her and I feel their judging stares.

My brother I avoid. It's this loss that I feel the most keenly. Why does he have to be so angry with me and distrustful of Raleigh?

I hate that his words haunt me day and night. Even though my husband has sworn to me that he loves me and will do all he can so we can live together as a couple out in the open.

I live for the morning when the maid brings me my letters. The one I long for is from Raleigh. I crack open the sealed letter. At the top is a little drawing of a buck. His name and mine are entwined with love knots. I smile to myself as I imagine him taking the time to sketch this out.

He writes that he is approaching Essex to try to garner more support for when he has to tell the queen. As her favourite, his words will hold more weight. Raleigh, who hates Essex, has decided to try to make peace with him in order to garner support for our cause. Once I am done reading his letter, I kiss it and feed it into the fire.

As March approaches, my brother's temper cools, and at my sister-in-law's insistence we dine together as a family.

We dine on roasted quail, thick stew, and custards.

The silence is palpable, but Lady Ann takes this as a good step forward.

"Have you planned out where the ditches will go to improve the drainage on the farms?"

Arthur grunts in reply. I have a feeling that if I looked up I would find him glaring at me, so I content myself with the food before me. These days I'm famished, and I pay no heed to the midwife that warns if I keep eating like this the baby will grow too big.

After dinner is carried away we retire to the chamber adjoining and enjoy a game of cards—well, Ann and I do. It takes a few games before Arthur joins us.

At last he breaks his evening-long silence with a loud sigh. "I worry for you."

I glance up from my cards to find him watching me with the most heart-wrenching sorrowful expression. My hand itches to reach across the table to his, but I don't want to interrupt.

"He should be taking better care of you. There are a lot of things he should be doing. I just cannot believe that he would lead you astray like this."

I blush, looking down at my lap. "We've been together for over four years. This wasn't the act of a single night. I am much more to blame than he is, truth be told."

He has turned a lovely shade of red to match my own.

"If you were angry because you thought he was some miscreant who took advantage of me, he was not. I—I didn't wish to marry him. Until. This." I point to my belly.

He is gaping, but when he recovers he asks, "Why ever not?"

"I wanted to be sure I loved him. I would not wish to be miserable or chained to a man who would be unfaithful or horrid to me once we were married."

"So you thought you'd try him out?" He claps a hand over his mouth, disbelieving the words coming out of his own lips.

"Not quite like that. Although plenty of men do it and no one seems to bat an eye when they follow their own desires. What I'm getting at is that you shouldn't hate Raleigh. I am just as guilty in this, but I am walking on the path I have chosen to take. No one forced me down this road."

"That reassures me somewhat," he says. "When I left you in London, I thought you'd be safe under the watchful eye of the queen."

I share a look with Lady Ann. Thankfully, my brother doesn't see it. Even in her day men and women were often sneaking off to have trysts.

"I will need time to let my temper cool. But, Bess, I don't hate you and I will never turn you out of this house. Never fear on that account."

I dab at the corners of my mouth. "I appreciate it."

My son Damerei arrives on a sunny day in early March. The labour, which was hard and arduous, is forgotten the minute I hold him in my arms. My brother has employed a wet nurse, but for his first feed I hold him to my own breast. Soon I will have to be parted from him. After I have recovered, I am to go back to court. Raleigh sends a man with gifts and letters the very day of his birth. He is away at Portland waiting for a strong wind to carry his fleet to Panama otherwise, he swears he would be at my side. While I have been away he has enjoyed the fruits of his labour, which culminated in being made an admiral at last. His first mission is to attack the Spanish fleet and sack the city.

I don't begrudge him staying away or his travels. My husband has never been the sort of man to sit still for long. I send him a letter in reply, saying both his son and I are well and wishing him Godspeed.

At my son's christening many of Raleigh's friends attend. The Earl of Essex arrives with his wife and I finally meet the famous Frances Walsingham. I had expected her to be a haughty, vain woman. Instead though she seems shy at first it's clear she has a razor sharp wit.

We take to each other like two peas in a pod forcing Essex to extend his visit at Coughton.

"I am so glad our husbands have put aside their differences," I say, rocking Damerei to sleep in my arms.

"We have this little one to thank." Frances smiles at my son.

"Do we?"

She nods. "I believe your husband, will move mountains for you. He was willing to put aside his enmity towards my husband."

"These men are always eager for war." I shake my head. "Damerei, you will be different won't you?"

He gurgles in response and we both laugh.

In April, I return to court missing the little cherub I left behind in the care of my brother. Essex, who stood as godfather at his christening, doesn't even look my way as I enter the queen's rooms and resume my duties as if nothing has happened.

"You look so well," Catherine Howard congratulates me. "I see a rest in the country has done you wonders."

"Thank you, Lady Catherine."

She smiles, but it doesn't reach her eyes. I begin more than ever to suspect she knows more than she is letting on. If I am being paranoid, I'd rather I don't expose myself.

Lady Holland rushes over too. "You've never looked better." She pulls me aside and whispers, "Which physician did you see? I should like to know if I ever find myself ill. He has done wonders for you."

I cough awkwardly and promise to tell her. "My brother arranged it all. I was ill, as you know."

She nods, understanding, and regards me with a look I can only call pitying. I can't help but feel a pang knowing I've lied to a good person who's always looked out for me.

The days begin to blend together with monotonous fashion. Of course there are comments or wide-eyed stares, but no one says anything. Perhaps I am being foolish to hope that all will be well, but when a letter arrives from my brother saying that the Lord Chamberlain came to interrogate him about Damerei's parentage, I know it is only a matter of time before a storm breaks over our heads.

In a moment of fear, I write to my brother to have Damerei and his wet nurse sent to Durham House. Raleigh is due to return any moment. His half-brother is there overseeing his affairs and knows about his nephew's existence. I don't want to drag my family into my affairs any further than I already have.

With no discreet way to get a message to Raleigh, I simply flee court and head for Durham House, meeting my son and nurse on the way.

He is home. Thank God he is home.

I weep into his jacket as Raleigh removes our son from my arms, passing him to the nurse, and wraps me up tight. He motions for the nurse to leave us alone and waits until she is out of the room before speaking.

"Hush now, my love. We knew this was bound to happen," he says, putting on a brave face.

"I know," I say, forcing myself to stop sobbing uncontrollably. "What will the queen say when she finds out?"

Raleigh kisses my temple. "I shall go to her in the

morning. If I have the chance to speak to her alone, then we have a chance."

"If not?"

"We deny everything."

"What?" I pull back, though I desperately miss his warmth.

"Deny everything. Who knows what lies my enemies have whispered to her? She might be poisoned against us. So we deny we ever saw each other."

I shake my head. No. "And Damerei? Was he wished into being?"

He steadies me. "You and I know the truth of how things stand between the two of us. The rest is all for show. We just need to get the queen to approve."

"But..."

He kneels before me, clasping my hands together between his own and kissing them. "You are my life. I would not ask you this if I didn't think it was absolutely necessary. I have a plan, and if all works out, then we shall be together at Durham House raising our son."

"All right. But I shan't bastardise our son. He was born in wedlock."

"Let's hope you aren't questioned too closely."

We retire to bed together, our son laid out in his crib beside us. Neither of us sleep well, but we are content to be together.

In the morning, I must return to court.

I am not there long before Heneage, one of her majesty's trusted councillors, pulls me aside and invites me to take a turn about the palace gardens with him.

"I am afraid I cannot," I say with a smile. "The queen—"

He interrupts me. "Would very much like it if you came with me."

I swallow hard. We have been caught.

At first all we do is walk. Then he invites me to sit on a bench. My back is straight as a needle as he begins to ask questions about dates and times I have been gone from court.

"Sir, I do not recall." This isn't even a lie. I didn't keep track of dates when I slipped away to meet with Raleigh, and perhaps this is a good thing, all things considered. "I was often doing something in the queen's service. If I was away, it was usually to be with my brother at his house. You may ask him if you wish."

"We have and we will ask him again," Heneage says, which is not a comfort to me. I fret over the safety of my family and fidget in my seat.

"The sooner you confess your sins, the sooner this can end. You can return home, and perhaps the queen will grant you forgiveness."

I hide my face from his view as best I can and don't say a word. My hands clench around the fabric of my dress. My faults are that I love a man, but I will do as my husband bid me and deny everything. When I look up at him, my expression is serene and defiant.

His smile vanishes and he nods. "We will get to the bottom of this one way or another. You are to be placed under house arrest until this matter is concluded."

Now that my worst fear has come to pass, I find I am

not afraid. I stand, knowing it would be pointless to protest or try to run. Calmly, I follow him and allow two guards to escort me away.

Orders for our transfer to prison are written and signed, but our friends are working hard behind the scenes to prevent this from coming to pass.

Our momentary reprieve ends abruptly when I am rowed upriver by barge to the tower.

I don't see my husband all this time and have not been able to hear a single word, but I lay my trust in him and pray that we shall be reunited soon.

Being a gentlewoman means I am afforded certain comforts. My room has a threadbare carpet, a writing desk, and a feather mattress. They bring plenty of blankets in for me and three plain dresses. A maid will look after my needs and stoke the fire in my chamber. I am grateful, but boredom threatens to make me go insane.

Heneage comes in and asks me if I gave birth to a son.

"You may see him if you wish. If, that is, you have a son," he says.

I falter and cannot bring myself to deny his existence. I give him a nod, and he smiles and makes a mark on his paper. "And what of the boy's father? Who is he?"

Now that I've already acknowledged my son and I am already here in the tower, I don't know what else I have to gain by denying him.

"My husband."

Heneage smirks and shakes his head. "His name, my lady. I need his name."

"Sir Walter Raleigh." My heart sinks into my stomach.

Two months go by and Lady Ann is allowed to bring my son to visit me. She comes in carrying a basket filled with books for me to read and writing paper.

"I am sorry I couldn't do more for you," she says as she lays out the items she brought for me. "I was allowed to bring you the paper but not ink."

I laugh, which makes Damerei smile. Turning back to my son, I coo at him and tickle him underneath his chin. He's the sweetest thing.

"He has grown so much," I say, trying to push down the pang of resentment that I cannot have him with me.

"He eats so much," she says. "His wet nurse complains night and day."

I smile. "Good. And how are you? Your baby?" For I see her stomach is flat once more.

"Another girl," she says. "We've named her Abigale after my mother. I know Arthur doesn't complain, but I hope we shall have a son as well. Just to break the cycle."

I laugh. "Well, you have Damerei to practice on in the meantime."

"We are taking good care of him," Lady Ann assures me. She can guess better than anyone else how I am feeling being separated from my child like this.

"I know, and I am grateful. What news do you have for me?"

She opens her mouth to answer, but there's a knock at the door and the guard sticks his head in the door.

"Time to go, my lady," he says to Lady Ann.

As she leans to kiss my cheek in farewell, Lady Ann whispers, "Raleigh's ships have captured a Spanish ship. They are returning to England. Pray it contains enough loot to tempt the queen."

The sound of my heart pounding in my ears is all I can hear as my sister-in-law and son disappear out the door.

A week goes by and there is no news. At least none for me but I sense a shift. Ink appears on my writing desk and I'm invited to send letters to my family and friends. Of course all of the letters will be read and studied to ensure I am not sending coded messages. I roll my eyes. Any secrets worth hiding they have already uncovered, but I am grateful for the chance to write.

Lady Ann visits me again. She doesn't have my son in tow but reassures me his father has taken him to his house.

"What?" I think I have misheard her.

"There is plague in the city. He thought it best to send him to the country with his wet nurse."

"But my husband, you said...he is free?"

She looks confused as to why I haven't been told. "Yes, three days ago the queen released him so he might sort out the affair with the cargo of the Spanish ship." She stops herself with a wave of her hand. "It's a complicated mess. He offered the queen a fortune in exchange for his freedom. She capitulated."

"I see." I am breathless. "And for me?"

Lady Ann looks away. "The queen says since you continue to claim Raleigh is your husband, she cannot countenance setting you free."

"And what does *he* have to say about it?" I linger over the word.

Lady Ann's cheeks turn a dusty rose. "He signed everything the queen demanded of him."

"So he has denounced me?"

"From what I heard he denied he ever spoke to or married you."

Her words sting like the lash of a whip.

Deny. Deny. Deny. That is what Raleigh said we should do. He reminded me that his words did not matter because the oath between us was unbreakable. I couldn't bring myself to be a Judas, so I am here behind bars with no hope of escape while he is free out there. No doubt waiting for me.

Lady Ann pats my back. I look up, surprised to find my cheeks wet with tears.

"We are doing our best for you. Raleigh cannot speak out publicly for you. He has denied you and sworn to the queen he is loyal to her and her alone. His freedom was given on this condition and would be forfeited if he asked for your release. If it's any consolation, he bade me bring you this," she says, slipping me a thin slip of paper she had tucked away in her sleeve.

Inside is a short poem.

Her eyes fixed upon me
The dimples of her smile dazzled
But her mind entrapped
He would have her know
He'd be true to the last
If only for a kiss
And a stolen moment.

I throw it into the flames. "If you see him, tell him it's very sweet, but I'd rather he be here in person to read it to me himself."

Lady Ann leaves me alone with my thoughts. I am given more liberty now that Raleigh is freed, and every day a guard comes to take me out for a walk along the tower green.

I long to be like the ravens and soar above the clouds.

CHAPTER 10

1593

Four months after Raleigh's release, the queen finally relents and signs an order for my release.

I hope to never be within the stone walls of the tower again.

My brother waits for me outside the gates with an escort to take me to Sherborne Castle.

"They are waiting for you there," he says to me. "I am happy to see you have come out of this unscathed."

We are outside London before he turns to me.

"Do you still love him?"

"I should hate him for not storming the tower to free me from my prison. But Arthur even after all this time my heart yearns for him. I'm a fool in love," I say and then laugh. He must think I am half mad. But I am filled with such elation that now we may face the future together, side by side as man and wife.

As our retinue reaches the outskirts of Sherborne I see a cloud of dust being kicked up. I pull on the reins of my horse to bring him to a halt and squint my eyes to see who is riding toward us.

I nearly shout out when I see that it is Raleigh on his dark charger coming toward me like some handsome knight or rather a devil coming to seduce me.

He pulls up beside me and leaps from his horse. His eyes searching mine for any sign. When I smile, he returns it and pulls me from the saddle to embrace me before beginning to shower me with kisses.

Only the cough from my brother stops us. Raleigh, looking coy, apologises for his enthusiastic greeting. Then he turns to me. "I have long dreamed of this moment," he whispers in my ear.

We arrive at the castle gatehouse and we dismount. Grooms lead our horses away and I am greeted by the sight of our child waiting in the arms of his nurse.

My vision is blurry from tears, but I hold them back. I have shed enough tears to last me a lifetime. From now on only laughter and smiles will fill my days.

My brother and his wife stay for a feast to welcome me home. My new house is filled with strangers toasting my arrival and showering me with compliments due to the lady of the house. Having been alone for so long, I am taken aback to be surrounded by so many people, but with Raleigh's steadying hand at my back I am content.

~

That evening I am getting dressed for bed when Raleigh enters and sends away my maids.

"I could not bring myself to deny you or our child. Have you come to admonish me for not obeying your instructions after we were arrested?"

He doesn't speak but shakes his head.

Sheepishly, I watch him from the corner of my eyes as he approaches. When his hands run over my exposed skin, I shudder. His hands make quick work of the laces of my gown. But he is meticulous in his slow deliberate movements as he removes layer after layer of clothing.

I am in my shift and I think he shall remove this too, but instead he retreats from the room and returns with a nightgown etched with silver thread and beaded pearls.

"A gift fit for the queen of my heart." He offers it to me on bended knee. "This and many more sumptuous gifts that I will lay at your feet until I have earned your forgiveness."

I could tease him, prolong his suffering, but after months without his touch I am impatient.

"I need only you." I push aside the nightgown. "And what of me? Will I be enough for you?"

He grins. "What sort of question is that?" His eyes flick from me to the bed beyond.

"Prove it," I challenge him.

A squeal of surprise escapes me as he sweeps me into his arms and carries me to the foot of the bed as if I was weightless.

My body arches against his as he deposits us on the

bed. We are swallowed up by the soft mattress and our pleasure.

"If I had denied our marriage," I begin to say into the darkness of our room.

But he hushes me.

"It's in the past. There is no reason to dwell on it now."

"I want you to know. Though I didn't listen to you, I still trusted you. Lady Ann told me you had denied I was your wife and swore to the queen you were loyal to her alone. But I never wavered in my belief that you loved me. I'm sure many thought I was a fool."

He shuffles over to me, pulling me into his arms. "You a fool? Ha. Preposterous."

"And what makes you the judge?"

He chuckles. "Well, you see, my dear, I am the King of Fools. I would recognise you at once if you were one of my subjects."

"Perhaps you cannot—"

"Why?" he asks sleepily.

"Because I am the Queen of Fools."

He tickles me until I am left screeching.

"You will bring the servants running. They will think we are being assassinated in our bed."

He hums. "Not a bad way to go, all things considered."

I glower at him, though he cannot see me in the dark.

"I am still not eager to be embarrassed like this on my first night as mistress of this castle."

The sleep has gone out of him as he strokes my face. "I will make amends."

I cannot know for certain, but I like to imagine that our second son, Walter, was conceived on that very night. He is the very image of his father. Watching our children play freely in the gardens of Sherborne fills me with such joy. I know nothing can touch us here.

When I retreat inside to find my husband, I find him moving about his privy chamber with a restless energy that cannot be controlled. Once again, I am reminded that soon he will be sailing for the New World to find the mythical city of El Dorado. He is not gone, yet a fresh pang of sorrow hits me. The queen is funding this voyage, and I cannot help but wonder if it is to spite me. But no, I doubt she thinks of me.

When he first told me he was to go, I begged him to reconsider. Now I am resigned, knowing that he will return to me as he always does.

"Why so glum?"

Pulled out of my thoughts, I look up to see my husband standing before me, the corner of his mouth turned up in that half-smile of his.

"I will miss you," I admit. "The days will pass by so slowly while you are gone."

He chucks me under the chin. "Then you shall have to find ways to keep yourself busy."

"How?" I ask with all the irritability of a child.

He pulls me from the privy chamber with the chests laden with supplies to our bedroom. "Over there, above our bed on the ceiling, I would like a mural painted and the walls plastered. New furnishings top to bottom."

Raleigh continues on in this vein for quite some time, only stopping when he sees my incredulous face.

"Remodel, refurnish. All of it. The whole castle! That quaint little hunting lodge we stumbled across during one of our excursions." He wiggles his eyebrows. "Rebuild!"

I recall the crumbling walls and smell of rot even as I remember the rustle of our clothes as he pressed me up against a pillar, his lips crashing against mine in that delicious way.

"Hmm, I suppose. A good mattress there would be a good investment." I tap a finger against my cheek as if I'm deep in thought. My yelp, as he grabs me by the waist and spins me up in the air as if we are dancing a galliard, turns into a laugh.

He sets me down and steadies me with one hand as I stumble.

"You are incorrigible, Lady Raleigh."

"Insatiable," I correct him. "As befits a pirate lord's wife."

AUTHOR'S NOTE

Walter Raleigh journeyed deep into Central America. He never found the famed city of El Dorado, but he may have been the first European to find Angel Falls.

By all accounts, Bess and Raleigh led a happy harmonious life together. However, he was often away on his expeditions and never out of trouble with the law for long. Though their first son would perish before he reached maturity, they would have another son, named Carew.

During Queen Elizabeth's reign he was accused of being an atheist for promoting wild ideas such as Galileo's theory that the Earth revolved around the sun. One of the men who was to testify against him at his trial was the famous playwright Christopher Marlowe. The night before the trial Marlowe was murdered in cold blood. Many speculated that Raleigh had him killed to save himself. Regardless of the truth of this story, Raleigh managed to weasel out of trouble this time as well.

After Queen Elizabeth's death, Raleigh once again found himself imprisoned for plotting against the new King James I. Eventually, King James set him free and allowed him to travel for a second time to South America in search of El Dorado. While there, Raleigh ordered his men to sack the Spanish settlement, unaware that King James had just brokered a peace treaty with Spain. Upon his return to England, he found himself promptly arrested once more.

For a time he thought he might be freed. Alas, this time he was found guilty and the king signed his death warrant.

One of his last letters was to his wife, Bess which survives to this day. It spoke of his love for her and counselled her on how to manage without him.

The letter requests she looks after their sons. He offers her plenty of advice, including that she take God as her next husband, though he acknowledges that it might be more prudent for her to remarry. When I read this I was touched by his humour and sarcasm, and I used that as the basis for his character in this book.

Like most women of the era, not much is known about Elizabeth Throckmorton besides the references that survive in letters written by her brother and husband as well as the records of her arrest. While it is possible that Raleigh tricked and seduced her, there is every indication that she was a strong-willed woman who may have been the one to play the part of the seducer.

This story draws heavily from history, but I embellished a lot as well. Above all else, I hope that you enjoyed this story.

PREVIEW: READ NEXT...

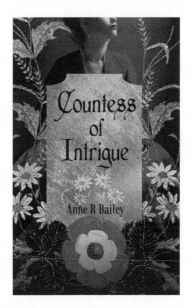

The story of Frances Walsingham, daughter of Elizabeth I's famous spymaster. Can be read as a standalone.

Chapter One

"Why do you think Penelope remained faithful to Odysseus all those years?"

It's late. I should be asleep, not trying to strike up a conversation with my old nursemaid. Outside, the storm has abated, leaving the world buried under an ocean white. Perched on my seat by the window, I am entranced by the beauty of it. The garden my mother dearly loves has disappeared. Tomorrow she will complain and I will try to appear sympathetic, but for now I long to press my forehead against the windowpane.

Behind me, Lady Anne Forrester stirs. "What kind of silly question is that? She remained faithful because that is what a good wife ought to do," she says. I don't have to look at her to know she's rolling her eyes.

All in all, she is the most backward woman I know. She may have been the one who taught me how to read and write, but she hates when I try to draw her into debates. She has no interest in plays, poetry, ballads, or even the English Bible. Nor does she discuss philosophers, politics, or the latest fashions. In fact, I suspect she's a secret Catholic. The way she clutches her book of psalms it might as well be a rosary. Maybe she used to be a nun. It's easy to imagine, as she certainly has the stern face for it.

My father would know. He knows everything about everyone. He's made a living out of knowing. We live in a house filled with nothing but secrets. They are the currency we use to keep clothes on our backs and our larders full. Any coin we have disappears into the pockets of hooded men, beautifully clad whores, and lowly page boys. My father runs the largest spy network in all of Europe. He knows everyone's secrets. But it's better to leave some stones unturned.

Lady Anne is warming her hands by the fire. There's a pang in my chest as I regard her. I can't imagine losing her company, Catholic or not.

I feel like a tragic figure out of antiquity, trapped by a cruel fate. I already miss my home and I haven't even lost it. Yet.

Penelope was like this, left to wait year after year for her husband's return. How did she feel when he didn't return to her even after the Trojan War had ended? Did she learn to accept her loneliness? Or maybe she preferred it.

"I imagine she liked being a widow, but when the suitors showed up, she had to play the part of the loyal wife waiting for her husband."

Lady Anne meets my gaze. Her face is taut with disapproval. "What put such terrible notions inside your head?"

"I'm just saying that it must have been nice to be the sole ruler of Ithaca..."

"She had a son, didn't she? Once he grew up he would inherit his father's kingdom. She was only safe-guarding his inheritance. And you saw what trouble a woman on her own attracts. Penelope was lucky her husband returned."

Lady Anne doesn't use the word *regent* to describe

Penelope, as that would give her power. But regardless of how people might try to diminish it, Penelope held power. For a time at least.

Then a thought strikes me and it's hard to keep from smiling. Despite her best efforts, it's clear Lady Anne has been paying attention as I read aloud. "I thought you didn't like the Greeks."

"Heathens," she says. The word comes out as a hiss. "I want nothing to do with them. Look at the ideas they've put in your head."

"Don't blame them. It's my silly mind that is at fault. As you have pointed out, Penelope is the perfect model of a loyal wife, even in this day and age."

"Go say your prayers. You should be in bed. Given my age, I should be in bed." Lady Anne shifts in her seat, but she isn't eager to leave the warmth of the fire.

"In a moment." I turn back to the window before adding, "What do you think it would be like to be out there right now?"

She snorts with derision. "Cold, you foolish girl."

She is right. Only a fool would love this icy barrenness. But I prefer it to all other seasons, especially because of what awaits me in spring: marriage.

To marry for the benefit of her family is the duty of every daughter, but it doesn't stop the feeling of dread from welling up in the pit of my stomach. Knowing your duty and actually doing it are two different things. It's not that I fear the wedding night. That business between a man and his wife does not make my toes curl. Nor does the thought of leaving my family home keep me tossing and turning all night. Not even the uncertainty of child-birth gives me pause.

No, it's him. My intended: Philip Sidney. Even now I can't think of him without my cheeks growing hot from embarrassment.

The last time we spoke my father had just informed me I was to marry him. Sidney was sitting to the left of my father at the dinner table and didn't even bother looking up from his fish.

Then my father had suggested rather calmly that now would be as good a time as any to sign the betrothal contract.

"I agree." Sidney yawned. "Your hospitality has been lavish as usual. Let's conclude this business so I may sleep."

I looked from him to my father, unable to compre-hend what I was hearing. "Why on Earth would you wish to marry me?" The question cut through the room, silencing all other conversation. My father fixed me with one of his infamous glares. I never felt so small.

It was Sidney who spoke first. "Lady Frances, I am marrying you so we might form a lasting alliance between our two families." He took his time over each word, leaving no room for any misunderstanding.

Perhaps he thought I was a simpleton. I certainly had not been able to keep my composure and was forced to focus on my hands, squeezed into tight fists in my lap.

Neither my intended nor my father said anything more to me and the pair of them, thick as thieves, left the room.

The memories are still painful to recall. Even my mother's comforting words did little to soothe my injured pride. I had made a fool of myself and I had seen the look of contempt on my future husband's face. If there was ever a good way to start a marriage, this was not it.

All I imagine when I think of Sidney is how he looks past me as if I am not there. When I grow accustomed to this thought my mind comes up with other scenarios, both real and imagined, that torment me. I see him laughing with all his friends at how silly I am, how incompetent. Will he turn away from me in disgust after we say our vows? I cannot imagine this man would ever cherish me.

Why must I marry him?

I pray for guidance as I never have before. He is my father's protégé, the son he never had. Since my father cannot legally make him his heir, he has married him to me, his only surviving daughter. It is a neat solution that benefits everyone but me.

The Sidney family is well regarded and sits high in the queen's favour. They are famous for being accomplished courtiers and scholars. That is intimidating enough, but they are also wealthy with an impressive family lineage that connects them to the dukes of this realm. Who am I but the daughter of a lowly knight?

Every day I hope that news will arrive from London that Sidney has changed his mind. Then every night as I lay my head down on my pillow I assure myself that tomorrow will be different. Tomorrow I will discover I am no longer betrothed.

It is ridiculous that no one asks me if I agree to the match. The priest might ask on the day of my wedding, but how could I say no and flee back down the aisle? Has anyone ever done such a thing? I recall there were sainted women who fled, but they usually suffered terrible fates and if they did not then they were still not free to do as they pleased.

The bride is an afterthought in this whole marriage business. The glue that seals the deal. And now I can vouch that it isn't a very pleasant experience. Even the promise of a new gown does nothing to cheer me.

"Lady Frances, are you well?"

Blinking, I see Lady Anne is at my side. She places a warm hand on my forehead. "I was just thinking."

"You are so pale and cold. If you catch your death, your father will hang me up by my feet. Come to bed now." Her voice is soothing. Her eyes soften as she regards me. There are many things that we don't discuss out loud. My deep unhappiness is one of them. I must stop this nonsense. How can I be afraid of such a little thing as marriage? Did my father not survive the St. Bartholomew massacres? Am I not his daughter? Giving her hand a gentle squeeze, I obey at last and slide away from the window.

"It wouldn't be by your feet. He would string you up by your wrists. It's just as painful, but you wouldn't die or pass out." In a house like mine, with a father like mine, you learn a thing or two.

She chucks me under my chin as if I was still a child. "Petulant as always."

The next day the sky is clear and the snow already shows signs of melting. The scullery maid has already been in my room, building up a fire against the cold that has seeped in overnight.

There might be time for me to slip down the stairs and out through the courtyard to the stables beyond. The roads might be clear enough for me to manage a ride, even if it's just around the manor grounds.

Just as I finish throwing a cloak over my shoulders there is a tap at my door. Lady Anne is still fast asleep. Sneaking out the back passage is tempting but foolish. There's really only one option.

Carefully, I open the door to reveal Master Sidwell standing there.

He bows his head respectfully to me. "Your father wishes to see you, Lady Frances," he says as he takes in the cloak tied around my neck. He will report to one of my parents what he has seen. There will be questions about what I'm sneaking out to do at this early hour. Or worse, if I'm meeting with someone.

It's almost thrilling to be suspected of something so illicit.

"Very well, where is he?" I ask out of habit. The answer is always in his study.

"I shall escort you, my lady." He bows again.

So he's decided I cannot be trusted. My father has all the people in his employ well trained. He never chooses people who are slow-witted or easily swayed by bribes—

though as he reminds me frequently, everyone has a price. He'd rather have a farmer's boy for his secretary than a gentleman's son if he's quick on his feet.

The air is crisp as we walk through the wood-panelled halls of Scadbury Hall. We pass by the portrait gallery occupied by only a handful of paintings. We are not an ancient family established here for generations, nor does my father wish to spend precious gold on something so frivolous.

By all accounts, Scadbury Hall is a welcoming house. We do not turn away travellers and show visitors every hospitality. We feed the poor from our kitchen—proper meals of thick stews and bread, not our table scraps.

My father, who does not believe in waste, will often find employment for these unfortunate souls. He believes, and rightfully so, that it is the duty of a landowner to look after his tenants. A country that cannot look after its poorest inhabitants is not one that can thrive.

He holds the unpopular belief that given the opportunity, anyone has the potential to rise to greatness. We only have to look to our own family history to know this is true. A few generations back we were nothing more than merchants. Even just a few years ago, my father was forced to flee England to escape the Catholic queen and her inquisition. She would have burned all of England down if God didn't intervene and bring Queen Elizabeth to her throne. In a reversal of fortune, my father is now one of her advisors, working every day on making sure the Catholic pope never holds sway in England again.

He loves England and, by extension, the queen so fully there is room for no other in his heart. I am certain she doesn't have a more devoted servant than him. Even so, she often holds him at arm's length and he, desperate for her acknowledgment, continues to do more to prove he is worthy of it.

I suppose that is our family's curse: we are doomed to misplace our affections.

You only have to look at my mother to see this is true. She adores my father to the point of obsession. If he were to die before her, she would journey to the underworld to retrieve him, just like Orpheus did. Except she would not fail. Since they are both still alive and well, she spends her days tending to his every need and hanging on his every word. She waits for him to return her love while paradoxically believing she is unworthy of it. The fact that she has only borne him a daughter, me, torments her. She is never unkind to me, but I catch her frowning at me when she thinks I can't see. I am a constant reminder of her failure to be perfect.

Spiteful as my mind often is, I imagine telling her that even if she gave him ten sons, he wouldn't love her any more.

But that is ungrateful of me. She is hurting as I am hurting.

As I have said, my family is cursed to look for love in the wrong place. That is why I am left pining for their affection. It is an old wound I have learned to live with. After all, I've had a lifetime to grow accustomed to being forgotten by my parents, as if I was a stray afterthought they accidentally wished into being one day.

We arrive at the door that leads to my father's office. Master Sidwell does not bother to knock and instead holds the door open for me.

My eyes need time to adjust to the brightly lit room. We spend a fortune every month on just the candles and lights in this room. My father, economical and calculating, keeps beehives on our property and has our own servants make the candles. He has oil lamps imported from as far as Constantinople.

Many like to imagine he works away like a spider in the dark making its web. Seeing this lavish room would spoil their fun.

"Good day, daughter," he says, getting to his feet.

I bow deeply. "Good morning."

"I am sorry to have interrupted your day. Your mother has spoken to me about ordering you a new gown and making general preparations for the nuptials." He begins what I suspect will be a long speech. As he talks his eyes are trying to pry my mind open for his inspection. I stay very still. "I am afraid I cannot allow it."

He pauses, expecting me to say something. I am uncertain what he wants me to say. But I know as well as him that if there's no money for such finery then there is none. I am as economical as an alehouse wife. Even though I may be young, I'm not the sort to cry over baubles and silks.

"Do you want a drink?" He invites me to sit as if we were equals sitting down to discuss the terms of a contract. My curiosity is piqued, but drawing up the rear is my fear of some recent development.

"No, thank you." Gracefully, I lower myself onto a wooden stool with a worn padded seat.

"Very well. There is no easy way to say this. You are a good daughter to me—you will understand. We cannot make preparations for a wedding or be seen to."

Hope flares and then quickly dies in my throat only to be replaced by a growing anxiety. I feel myself drawn into the spider's nest.

"Oh."

"I hadn't meant to involve you in this."

But he did.

"You will have to marry Sidney in secret. The queen does not approve or would not approve of the union. But we will press on and she will come around. Eventually."

And what if she does not?

The tightness in my chest is growing. My breaths are coming in shallower, and I fear I may faint. To stop myself, I dig my nails into my palms until I fear they have drawn blood.

"You might have to beg for forgiveness from the queen. She will understand. Play the part of the love-struck young woman."

Why would I want to play a part in this charade?

Finally, I cannot continue to sit here as meek as a mouse. "But I do not love him. If the queen would hate this marriage so much, then I do not want to go through with it." I get to my feet, clenched fists at my waist.

He approaches me slowly, his gaze disarming in its sincerity. My father takes my hand in his.

"This is greater than me or you. This is for England's benefit. Bad advisors mislead the queen. I need a strong ally bound to me by more than an oath."

"So you would offer me up to the gods as Agamemnon did his only daughter."

The corners of his eyes crinkle. "I am not asking for your life."

You might as well be. The faintness leaves me and now I am seeing red.

"But you would still see my blood shed."

He does not scold me for such vulgar talk. Gently, he pries my fist open and looks at the wounds inflicted there. He pulls out a handkerchief and bandages my hand. Then he moves on to my other, working with the efficiency and skill of a surgeon. Then, when he is done, he embraces me, enveloping me in the scent of pine, lavender, and horse. The smell of home.

"I know this isn't what you want. But it is your duty and I will demand you perform it both for me as your father and for your country. Sidney will be a kind husband. I would not give you to a cruel man. You can have all the clothes and jewels you deserve as a new bride after your marriage."

"You know I don't care about such things." I pull away. "Can't I—" But I cannot finish what I have to say. All he is asking is that I play along. A secret marriage would be preferable. I wouldn't have to put up with people fussing over me and teasing me. But maybe there's a chance this whole thing doesn't have to happen.

"If this marriage displeases the queen, she might send you both away from court. Your careers would be over."

He tilts his head, considering me with something akin to admiration. "It's a risk we are prepared to take."

The conversation is over. I don't have the stomach for a fight.

The urge to go outside and ride around the countryside has left me. Weary and emotionally drained, I retreat upstairs to my private apartment. As I enter, Lady Anne is busy scolding the maid for making my bed incorrectly. According to her standards the bedcovers are not straight enough.

She stops when she sees me and arches an eyebrow. The poor maid bobs a curtsy, grateful for the interruption.

"Where did you run off to this morning?"

"My lord summoned me." The bile is still in my throat. I cannot bring myself to call him father.

Her gaze travels to my bandaged hands and her brows furrow but doesn't ask. She drops the matter and returns to ordering the poor maid around while I sink into my seat at the window.

We go to the little chapel, hear mass with the entire household, and then return to break our fast in private. Cheese, fresh bread, and mincemeat pies are served to us on platters of silver gilt. My appetite surprises me. When my stomach feels like it might burst, I recline in my seat and sigh, as content as a barn cat.

"Shall we attempt to go for a walk?" Lady Anne suggests, not looking up from her plate.

She's doing me a kindness. I know how much she despises the cold. She is at least ten years older than my mother, who just turned forty, and I know how her joints creak and ache this time of year.

"I shall order the stable master to prepare the sled. We can go for a drive and hide under thick furs and blankets."

She nods.

It's mid-afternoon by the time we are bundled into the sled. The driver clicks his tongue and the horses set off. They are heavy workhorses meant for the plough, but now they are transformed into strong majestic creatures by the matching harnesses decorated with bells. The harnesses were sent from Germany, as was the green blanket hemmed with white fur on my lap. My father's Protestant friends have not forgotten him.

It's a mild winter day, but now that we are moving at such a fast speed the wind whips at my face. The chill is pure bliss.

"What happened to your hands?" Lady Anne asks at last as she takes my hands in hers.

"Some foolishness on my part. Nothing more. I hurt myself by accident. The wedding is to go ahead. That is what he wanted to talk about. Don't worry about me. I am completely resigned to it." Lady Anne doesn't need to know that the queen doesn't approve of this marriage. I'm doing this to protect myself as much as her. If they ever questioned her, she will truly be ignorant. But would it matter? The thought sends a fresh shiver down my spine.

"Are you indeed?"

I can tell from her tone she finds this hard to believe, so I do my best to appear nonchalant.

"He's a good man. I am lucky my father has made me such a good match. With time I'll adjust. I don't have any real objections." I am doing my best to convince us both.

She doesn't comment. After an hour we are forced to return, and I leave Lady Anne to warm herself by the fire.

I shake off my cloak, running a hand over the dark grey wool. My maid waits to pack it away in one of my chests, but I send her for some warm ale instead. The sprigs of dried lavender are displaced as I tuck the cloak away, breathing in deep as the scent wafts up.

We don't have long to dawdle. My mother expects me to join her every day for sewing and reading with her ladies. Today is one of those rare days when we don't have guests and we are left to entertain ourselves. Before I go to her rooms I remove the bandages from my hands. The half-moon indents have already scabbed over, and with any luck she will not notice them.

Scadbury Hall is not a large sprawling place, so we don't have far to go. The doors of her privy chamber are left open. Her generously sized room has large south-facing windows that provide plenty of light throughout the day. Unfortunately, it also tends to get hot even in the depths of winter. A quick glance tells me my mother is not here. My eyes travel to the closed door at the other end of the room that leads to her private bedchamber and the beautiful closet where she has set up a small prie-dieu.

Taking advantage of the bright light, her ladies sit in a half-circle around one of the large windows as they continue their work embroidering the large tapestry. Each woman has her own little corner that she tends to with needle and thread. It's taken the better part of the year to get this far and there is still so much to go.

Marta, my mother's favourite lady, is the first to spot me and gets up without a word to fetch me a chair. Margery Agote, my mother's impoverished niece, invites me to pick which part I would like to work on. Everyone is watching me, soft smiles on their lips. As tempted as I am to know where my mother is, I hold back the question and sit.

They ask me what I've been doing and comment on my pretty dress. It strikes me how attentive everyone is to me. A conspiracy of kindness. This silent show of support reminds me I'm not alone. My mood lightens considerably. I could laugh at how easy it is to get lost in my thoughts.

I settle on the brilliant blue used for the sky and thread the needle. It's mindless work. A balm that silences any new turbulent thoughts.

In time my mother joins us. There is something about her stiff posture, the redness in her eyes, that catches my attention. She's been crying. I cannot imagine it's over me. But later after we stop our work to eat and drink, she pulls me into her bedroom and closes the door behind her.

"What is it, Mother?" I cannot stand the anxiety of waiting. I was never a patient sort of person and over the last few weeks, any patience I have learned has eroded away.

She sniffs. "I know your father has spoken to you."

"Yes. He has."

"It's not his fault."

"I never said it was."

She paces the length of her room. "He keeps embroiling himself in plots. He needs help. Goodness knows the queen still sits on her throne because of him. The number of assassinations he has saved her from—" She cuts herself off. Even now, just between the two of us, she will not divulge state secrets. "But I thought he wouldn't involve you." She approaches me now. I almost want to take a step back. "You don't deserve to be dragged into this. Especially not to lose your chance for a respectable marriage."

"I thought you said this was a wonderful match for me."

She frowns. Melancholic and worried like this, my mother shows her age and more.

"I didn't think it would be like this for you. So much can go wrong. It would ruin your reputation if..."

"You mean if the queen decides that the marriage never happened? She's done it before, making a whore out of her own cousin, Katherine Grey. So why would she hesitate to have my marriage put aside if she despises it so much?"

My mother's breath hitches. I might have a reputation for being flighty and letting my mind wander, but I am not my father's daughter for nothing. I have inherited that knack for guessing people's thoughts from him.

"Mother, he knows this. Father will have made sure that the marriage will hold. He was the one who dismantled Katherine Grey's marriage, was he not? He will know how to protect me. We must trust him."

My words shock her. Flustered, she twists the belt around her waist in her hands. "I never said I didn't trust him. I worry for him. That is all."

How is it that it falls to me to comfort her? But I do it willingly. I take her hands in mine and squeeze them.

"It will be fine. I don't want a big ceremony, anyway. Nor do I need presents and congratulations. If I can make the two of you proud and be of some use, then I am content."

At last she smiles. "Who gave you such good sense? Still, if this goes wrong for him. Frances, you must do your best for him. Come what may, you must never betray this family. Even if the queen locks you away in the tower."

"I wouldn't," I say, and I mean it. Besides, the queen's best interrogator happens to be my father. Only he could have made Katherine Grey, pregnant with her first child, agree that she was never married and that the man she loved had raped her. He is not only a spymaster but also a conjurer, drawing words and confessions out of people.

So I don't fear anyone else. Not even William Cecil, who uses his sweet countenance and condescension to whittle out your private thoughts only to use them against you.

"Your father takes such risks upon his shoulders." My mother shakes her head. "He sacrifices so much."

I cannot help but grit my teeth. Of course her primary concern is him.

Her expression is serious as she studies our entwined hands. "I will make sure this isn't some silly business conducted in the dark."

"But I think that's exactly what Father wants. This marriage is supposed to be a secret."

She pulls her hands out of my grip. "There's a difference between being discreet and being vulgar. I wouldn't want anyone to say you gave yourself to him or eloped." She cups my face and kisses both cheeks.

"Be a good girl," she says, as if I am a child of five.

I nod because I do not trust myself to hold my tongue. I return to my needle and thread and the comfort of knowing that I am not the first woman to marry to please her family.